# THE PERSISTENCE OF MEMORY

A WAKE FOREST STUDIUM BOOK

*Pro Humanitate*

# THE PERSISTENCE OF MEMORY

## ORGANISM, MYTH, TEXT

Philip Kuberski

University of California Press
*Berkeley · Los Angeles · Oxford*

University of California Press
Berkeley and Los Angeles, California

University of California Press
Oxford, England

Copyright © 1992 by The Regents of the University of
California

Library of Congress Cataloging-in-Publication Data

Kuberski, Philip.
    The persistence of memory : organism, myth, text /
    Philip Kuberski.
        p.      cm.
    Includes bibliographical references and index.
    ISBN 0-520-07909-4
    1. Memory (Philosophy)   2. History—
Philosophy.   3. Natural history—Philosophy.   I. Title.
BD181.7.K83    1992                          92-19844
128'.3—dc20                                  CIP

1  2  3  4  5  6  7  8  9

*for Claudette*

# Contents


Introduction   1

1.  Unconscious Cities   5

2.  Dreaming of Egypt   20

3.  Inmost India   42

4.  The Word of Galaxy   60

5.  The Metaphor of the Shell   78

6.  The Memory of Nature   94

7.  Proust's Brain   115

8.  The Silence of Rivers   131

Notes   135

Index   143

# Introduction

I began writing this book without knowing it. After a summer in Europe I came back to California and wrote out a few essays about cities and museums and antiquity. I began to wonder at the power that a fresh encounter with ancient things had on me. Walking in Rome and Arles, I had begun to think about what memory is and why it is such a consolation and a mystery.

Anyone who has lived, off and on, in the commercial wastes of southern California—where in the course of a decade a series of different buildings or forms of buildings can appear on the same site—will have a sense of absolute otherness and familiarity when walking through such ancient cities. Los Angeles may not be as old as Arles, but when a branch library burns down or an apartment building is flattened it enters into the mind and into the unconscious, along with everything, whether romantic or banal, that only exists in fragments and traces, in memory.

Soon my interest in memory broadened from cultural to natural topics. I began thinking about the most basic of human mnemonics, things like stars and shells, and wondered why they play such an important role in human imaginings. In turn I began to reflect on the role that the natural world plays in lending form and consequence to our ideas of the self, of conscience, of a poem, and of scientific or mythological accounts of human origins. From there I explored the claims made by biologists and neurologists about how organisms organize themselves and how the brain is able to collect, store, and recollect memories.

The essays in this book became focused on the nature of

memory as it manifests itself in organisms, mythologies, and texts, and also on the way these three elements are reflected in one another. Although there is an order and a consistent point of view in these essays, I have not attempted to provide a consecutive or cumulative argument. My purpose rather has been to dramatize and illustrate the ways in which memory functions through associations, leaps, or other dislocations out of time or space and how the more profound of these occurrences can give us a new understanding of our relation to the world.

Thus a number of these essays are concerned with experiences of the sublime reported by Freud, Napoleon, and Erwin Schrödinger, with dreams recalled by Wordsworth and Descartes, and with sudden reflections described by Robert Oppenheimer, Kant, and Marcel Proust. Experiences of this kind make a new knowledge of the unconscious possible, if we understand by the unconscious more than simply the repressed elements of our mental life. Erwin Schrödinger believed that the unconscious included everything that our bodies do without our conscious knowledge. Respiration, heartbeat, digestion are not only autonomic processes but also forms of the unconscious. Given that the organism is an evolutionary outgrowth of the past, Jung believed that the individual unconscious was characterized by collective or archetypal forms which are expressed in dreams, mythology, and art. And Proust believed that involuntary memory could provide access, not only to the unconscious and the past, but to the principles of "literary production" enunciated by the living world.[1] From organisms through myth and into texts, one can see the persistence of the unconscious and of memory.

Western individuality and subjectivity come into being, as J. H. Breasted argued with regard to Akhenaton, when men and women achieve "the ability to forget." This heretic Pharaoh was the "first individual in history" because he was able to turn his back on "the drift of tradition" and replace the profligacy of polytheistic culture with a monotheism symbolized by the sundisk, "Aton."[2] According to this modern and Western perspective, the adventures of subjectivity begin with two fundamental acts: withdrawal from natural flux, and the association of the abstract with the divine. Both of these acts require the profound forgetting of which Breasted spoke, the wearying but heroic repression which gives us notions of our tragic or existential or poignant ephemerality.

In the essays that follow I explore the interplay of forgetting and recollecting in a number of different contexts. The first three essays concern Europe's relationship with antiquity and the East. Drawing on archaeology, psychoanalysis, and modernist poetry, "Unconscious Cities" focuses on the ways in which modern and ancient cities can represent one another in the unconscious. "Dreaming of Egypt" shows how modern philosophy, psychoanalysis, and cinema reveal "Egypt" in particular, and the non-European world in general, as a repository for forgotten or denied desires. And "Inmost India" develops this premise by exploring the ways in which, following the recognition of Sanskrit's relationship to Greek and Latin, Europeans have considered the antiquity and wisdom of India in relation to Western science and modern culture.

The next two essays push beyond antiquity to consider the sublime or unsettling effects that any prolonged contemplation of natural artifacts may have. "The Word of Galaxy," ranging from astronomy to Kantian ethics, and from Plato's metaphysics to science fiction, elaborates on the fundamental bond which human beings have imagined between some inner aspect of themselves and the spectacle of the stars. "The Metaphor of the Shell" takes this marine artifact as a natural metaphor which mediates the passage from the inorganic to the organic world and links the languages of mathematics and poetry, showing parallels between evolution and literature.

The last three essays explicitly consider the ways in which nature manages to remember itself. "The Memory of Nature" shows the ways in which neo-Darwinian theory and practice derive from a venerable tradition going back to Genesis, and opposes to it the highly speculative argument, offered by Rupert Sheldrake, of "formative causation." "Proust's Brain" further explores the traditionally physical and writerly assumptions about memory formation, moving from primitive,

Christian, and scientific examples, and then shows ways in which both Proust's novels and speculation by prominent physicists and neurologists provide an alternative. The book ends with "The Silence of Rivers," a brief reflection on the role of oblivion in natural, cultural, and personal memory.

* * *

I would like to thank Allen Mandelbaum for putting me in touch with Stanley Holwitz of the University of California Press. Working with Stanley, Rebecca Frazier, and Deborah Birns has been a pleasure. I would also like to thank Dennis Foster, Nina Schwartz, Alex Gelley, Fred Dolan, Dillon Johnston and Jim Hans for their encouragement and friendship, my brother Les for urging me on, and Claudette Sartiliot for all of these things, and more.

Several of the chapters in this book were originally published, in different forms: *The Georgia Review*, Winter 1990 ("Unconscious Cities"), *SubStance*, Volume 60 ("Dreaming of Egypt"), and *The Yale Review*, Autumn 1988 ("Proust's Brain"). My thanks to the editors of these journals for their interest in my work and permission to reprint.

Grateful acknowledgment is given to New Directions Publishing Corporation for permission to quote from the following copyrighted works: *The Personae* of Ezra Pound (Copyright © 1926 by Ezra Pound); H. D. (Hilda Doolittle), *Collected Poems, 1912–1944* (Copyright © 1982 by the Estate of Hilda Doolittle).

Grateful acknowledgment is given to Harcourt Brace Jovanovich, Inc., for permission to quote from the following copyrighted works: Excerpt from "The Waste Land" in *Collected Poems 1909–1962*, copyright 1936 by Harcourt Brace Jovanovich, Inc., copyright © 1954, 1963 by T. S. Eliot, reprinted by permission of the publisher. Excerpt from "Burnt Norton" and "East Coker" in *Four Quartets*, copyright 1943 by T. S. Eliot and renewed 1971 by Esme Valerie Eliot, reprinted by permission of Harcourt Brace Jovanovich, Inc.

# 1

## Unconscious Cities

Not to know one's way in a city doesn't signify much. But
to lose oneself in a city as one loses oneself in a forest calls
for schooling.

—Walter Benjamin

When the great cities of Europe and North America first began
to open their undergrounds to the traffic of municipal trains,
archaeological digs in the Near and Middle East had already
begun to uncover the boundary stones and broken walls of Troy,
Nineveh, and Babylon. As Paris, London, New York, and Berlin
became electrified, systematized, and plumbed, the cities of antiquity were brought to light for the first time in thousands of
years. But even before the digs of Heinrich Schliemann, Sir
Arthur Evans, and Robert Koldewey had substantiated myths
and legends from Homer and Genesis, Charles Baudelaire had
postulated that modernity was basically a perceptual faculty that
consisted of regarding a modern city—rising outward, upward,
and downward on the accumulated wealth of industry and empire—as if it were *already ancient*. To be modern, Baudelaire
implied, means to see one's life in a city like Paris poised on
the very edge of history, but also in eternity.[1]

As the languages and cities of Mesopotamia, Egypt, and the
Aegean became accessible to the electric lights of modern ar-
chaeologists, it became possible to consider ancient Babylon-
ians, Myceneans, and Trojans in an oddly familiar way. After
the devastations of World War I, Paul Valéry mused, "We later
civilizations . . . we too now know that we are mortal . . . Elam,
Nineveh, Babylon were but beautiful vague names, and the
total ruin of those worlds had as little significance for us as

their very existence. But France, England, Russia . . . these too would be beautiful names."[2] Indeed, as European culture began to feel a strange interest in, and identify with, the fallen cities of Mesopotamia and the Nile, a different light was cast on its own cities, both classical and modern. Athens and Rome could never have the same authority after the uncovering of Knossos and Babel: it was as if the very ground beneath them were crumbling.

Such reflections were by no means rare in the early decades of this century. Ezra Pound's classic imagist poem "In a Station of the Metro" perfectly expresses this uncanny modernity. Pound describes in two lines the appearance of passengers from a Parisian subway:

> The apparition of these faces in the crowd;
> Petals on a wet, black bough.[3]

But who or what has emerged from the underground? The faces are compared abruptly to petals on a bough, a simple enough analogy: people return from the darkness of the underground in the same way that flowers in spring return to wet boughs. But what can the petals themselves be compared to? According to the *Homeric Hymns*, flowers return as Persephone does from the underworld after Dis has released her from her autumn and winter imprisonment. Pound witnesses the return of the feminine—associated with organic renewal—out of the modern, and perhaps masculine, hold of technology. The subway in Pound's poem is the medium that leads to and from the underworld, the chthonic realm of elemental forces that regulate the basic natural cycles. In the unnatural light of the Metro with its white tiles and neat signs there is a meeting of history and eternity, modernity and myth.

One of Freud's last articles, "A Disturbance of Memory on the Acropolis" (1937), serves as a dramatic illustration of how such a modern reorientation of time and timelessness takes place in mental life. Freud's "disturbance of memory," described in a public letter to Romain Rolland, had occurred more than thirty years before the article was published, during his first visit to Athens and the Acropolis. He reports that his initial reaction upon mounting that ancient inner city in 1904 was a nonsensical one: "So all this really *does* exist, just as we learnt at school!"[4] Freud explains how this reaction was, among other things, a denial of his own success, which contrasted so starkly with the humble experience and achievements of his father, who could never have come such a distance from Vienna.

Freud's denial manifested itself through a "feeling of derealization" (*Entfremdungsgefühl*) which overtook him at that moment as he ascended to the lofty site of Western rationality. Such feelings result from a conflict between empirical facts and unconscious associations. In an attempt to balance the demands of reality and the unconscious, the ego experiences various derealizing sensations which call into question either the reality of the real ("What I see here is not real") or the reality of the conflict ("I've been here before!"). To avoid either of these absurdities, Freud produced a compromise which implied that he had always doubted the existence of Athens ("So all this really does exist!"), but he could produce it only "at the cost of making a false statement about the past."

Was it indeed a false statement? What Freud doubted was not only the geographical existence of Athens in general and the Acropolis in particular; his doubts must have concerned surpassing his father's achievements, as well as surpassing and dishonoring the fathers of Western idealism and science, Plato and Aristotle. But if these unconscious thoughts found expression in that moment on the Acropolis, they did so because Freud had in fact always doubted that Athens (the capital of Western Thought) was "real."

Such is the impression one gets from *The Future of an Illusion* (1927), where Freud compares an unsubstantiated "faith" in the geographical existence of cities one has never visited, such as Constance and Athens, with the "teachings and assertions" of religion. At this point in his life he describes his visit to Athens this way:

> I was already a man of mature years when I stood for the first time on the hill of the Acropolis in Athens, between the temple ruins, looking out over the blue sea. A feeling of astonishment

mingled with my joy. It seemed to say: "So it really *is* true, just as we learnt at school!" How shallow and weak must have been the belief I then acquired in the real truth of what I heard, if I could be so astonished now! But I will not lay too much stress on the significance of this experience; for my astonishment could have had another explanation.[5]

As we have just seen, Freud would not offer such an explanation until 1937. One can appreciate Freud's tentativeness in 1927, for he then associated Athens not with the origin of reason, but with the "unsubstantiated assertions" made by religions. He may have recognized that the Parthenon and the Propylaea were real structures, but he may not have agreed that the Acropolis was the "real" foundation of Western values. Could any city (*polis*) indeed be so high (*acro*) as to rise above its mythological past? Was it this that Freud doubted?

Freud's "disturbance of memory" and Pound's imagist epiphany take place in unconscious cities which suddenly displace the obtuse force of real cities. These two kinds of cities cannot be securely distinguished or neatly integrated, because each exists in relationship to the other. One's experience of a city is, in other words, haunted by an unconscious counterpart: the Paris one has imagined, dreamed about, and planned to visit cannot be left at home. It comes along and constantly interferes with—and so organizes—the traveler's experience. A distinct stratification separates unconscious expectations and associations, the scattered experiences of the city, and the memories that we will continue to revise for ourselves and others. Thus, when one visits Paris for the first time, disappointment or familiarity is inevitable, and more severe feelings of *déjà vu* indicate a powerful confirmation of a long-held, unconscious idea. Such feelings could be compared to encountering a ghost—of oneself and of a city. In such moments of disorientation, one suddenly finds oneself on the streets of an unconscious city.

Like the simplest thing, a city can evoke the unconscious, but unlike most other things, it can also represent it with a complex of signs, streets, and architectures. In *Civilization and Its Discontents* (1930) Freud tentatively provides such a detailed model in the eternal city of Rome: "Now let us, by a flight of imagination, suppose that Rome is not a human habitation but a psychical entity with a similarly long past—an entity, that is to say, in which nothing that has once come into existence will have passed away and all the earlier phases of development continue to exist alongside the latest one."[6] He goes on to describe this unconscious city in which buildings from different epochs occupy the same space on a timeless site. Then, despite the attractiveness of the allegory, Freud rejects it as "an idle game" which serves only to demonstrate how far we are from understanding mental life by pictorial means. However cumulative its architectural "memory," the eternal city—or any city—is "*a priori* unsuited for a comparison of this sort."

But Freud may have been more satisfied with this comparison than he could admit because it involved a city that could be reached only "by a flight of imagination." On another occasion he chose to compare the unconscious to the so-called Mystic Writing-Pad,[7] (what we would call a "magic slate"), a device with an erasable surface placed above a wax tablet. Everything written *and* "erased" on the surface (consciousness) is conserved on the wax tablet (the unconscious). It is strange that Freud selected a child's toy to represent the relationship between the conscious and unconscious minds when "beneath" the toy, so to speak, lay another and perhaps more attractive model: the palimpsest. We may guess that Freud's reluctance arose because Baudelaire had already used this model to describe the brain in *Les Paradis artificiels*: "My brain is a palimpsest and so is yours, reader. Innumerable layers of ideas, images, feelings have fallen successively on your brain, as softly as the light. It seemed that each buried its predecessor. But none has in reality perished."[8] If Freud were to have combined Baudelaire's model of the mind with his own, he might have compared the unconscious to the series of "Troys" uncovered by Schliemann: a kind of municipal palimpsest.

Freud obviously liked the comparison of psychoanalysis to archaeology. He consistently compared the act of interpreting dreams to the decipherment of hieroglyphic writing. Like a philologist Freud broke the code of dreams, but he also discovered, beneath the superficial writing of consciousness and the hieroglyphics of the unconscious, a living remnant of the ancient past. In an 1895 lecture to the Society of Psychiatry and Neurology in Vienna, five years before the publication of his dream book, he described the parallels between psychoanalysis and archaeology:

> If his work is crowned with success, the discoveries are self-explanatory; the ruined walls are part of the ramparts of a palace or a treasure house; the fragments of columns can be filled out into a temple; the numerous inscriptions, which, by good luck, may be bilingual, reveal an alphabet and a language, and, when they have been deciphered and translated, yield undreamed-of information about the events of the remote past.[9]

Considering this romantic analogy between architectural and mental excavation, one begins to understand the thinking that led Freud to compare the fundamental psychic conflict to the ancient Greek tragedy of Oedipus. Like Schliemann, Freud could demonstrate, in opposition to modern skepticism, the literal "truth" of an ancient myth: Oedipus, Jocasta, and Laius continue to live in our unconscious.

It was in this vein that Baudelaire explained how a palimpsest might conceal a monastic legend beneath a chivalric tale and Greek tragedy beneath a legend. Baudelaire's sense that modernity consists of seeing simultaneously the historical and the eternal aspects of a great city anticipates Freud's claim that one can find them in one's own mind. Seeing through the surface of Paris—not toward its past, but toward its future antiquity—one would uncover Nineveh, just as one might find Thebes beneath Vienna.

As Freud's visit to the Acropolis indicates, this *seeing into* is more than a faded abstraction for a certain fundamental or profound *insight*. It actually happens. When Freud saw into Athens he experienced a "feeling of derealization," that is, he could no longer be sure that everything the cultural tradition had passed on was not a highly involved lie. *Déjà vu* can be regarded as a "positive" version of this disturbance of memory which asserts that a new experience has unaccountably happened before. In both cases one "sees into" one's own unconscious by doubting the reality or singularity of the experience one "knows" one is having. The city is momentarily eclipsed by a startling experience of the unconscious projected into its streets, its buildings, and perhaps even its name. Anyone who has suddenly been struck by the strangeness of a familiar name—London, New York, Los Angeles—has taken the first, faltering steps into this underground where social reality and the unconscious are in conflict.

Carl Jung tells in his memoirs of an even stranger encounter with the unconscious during a visit to Ravenna in 1933. After visiting the tomb of Galla Placidia, the dome of which is covered with a simple mosaic of blue stones containing gold crosses and a scatter of stars, Jung and a friend entered the baptistery. Jung was amazed to find mosaics where he had remembered only windows: "I was vexed to find my memory so unreliable."[10] One mosaic with which he was especially taken showed Christ holding out his hand to Peter as they walked upon the sea of Galilee. After Jung returned home he gave a lecture about baptism and the mosaics, drawing attention to the very real danger involved in such a sacrament. When he tried to acquire some photographs of the mosaics, he was told that they did not exist.

Jung believes that the experience was instigated by the state of mind that overtook him as he left the tomb of Galla Placidia. Her "fate and her whole being were vivid presences" to Jung, who had often wondered how this cultivated woman could have endured leaving Byzantium to live with a barbaric prince in Ravenna, a relatively provincial city. Seeking to explain this vivid hallucination, Jung claims his identification with Galla Placidia was so complete that she acted as his anima, an embodiment of the unconscious representing the contents of the past. Identifying with his anima's dangerous sea crossing and her own immersion in the rude life of fifth-century Ravenna, Jung had, as he explains, "a brush with those perils [of drowning and "real" baptism] which I saw represented in the mosaics." He could deal with the upsurge of unconscious material only by identifying so completely with his anima that he *saw* the dangers and opportunities that she had faced so long ago. The imaginary mosaics were a hallucinated compromise between, on the one hand, Jung's twentieth-century existence, and on the other, his unconscious identification with the Byzantine Empress and his internalized, psychic, feminine other.

One can appreciate why Jung's great desire to visit Rome was always tempered by apprehensiveness about the effects it was likely to have upon him. Sailing from Genoa to Naples in 1912, he came to the railing of the ship when it crossed the latitude on which Rome is situated. Jung recalls imagining the "smoking and fiery hearth" from which ancient cultures had emerged: there classical antiquity "still lived in all its splendor and ruthlessness." The same attraction and dread registered in these phrases about Rome could characterize his feelings of exultation and danger in Ravenna. Discussing Christ's singular effect on the Roman Empire, he refers to the "omnipresent, crushing power of Rome" which had "robbed" many diverse peoples of their "cultural independence." Now, Jung claims, we are faced with a similar threat of "being swallowed up in the mass" of modern society.

Unlike Paris or London, Rome was not a city that Jung could consider simply "visiting." He says, "If you are affected to the depths of your being at every step by the spirit that broods there, if a remnant of a wall here and a column there gazes upon you with a face instantly recognized, then it becomes another matter entirely." Such a visit would entail something very dangerous, a momentous tapping of the unconscious which he was unprepared to accept. When, as an old man, he had finally decided to go, he was stricken and fainted while buying tickets for the journey. He never again attempted the trip.

If Galla Placidia was the source of Jung's reaction to Ravenna, Freud may well have played a similar role in Jung's psychic relations with Rome. In 1897 Freud wrote to Wilhelm Fliess: "I dreamt I was in Rome, walking about the streets and feeling surprise at the large number of German street and shop names. I awoke and immediately realized that the Rome of my dreams was really Prague." In *The Interpretation of Dreams* Freud tells of his long-frustrated desire to visit Rome and of how his recurrent dreams nearly fulfilled this wish. In another dream Freud arrives in a "Rome" which is strangely rural. Faced with the difficulty of finding his way in a city he has never visited, Freud follows a dark stream and large white flowers. These transformations having removed the threatening antiquity of Rome, he discovers himself in "Ravenna," a city he had visited and which had for a time "superseded Rome as capital of Italy." It appears that Freud's unconscious could allow him only to visit the city which had succeeded or "surpassed" Rome.

In both *The Interpretation of Dreams* and his letters to Fliess, Freud offers as an explanation of his frustrated desire to visit Rome his childhood identification with Hannibal, the Semite general who attempted to conquer the city but never managed even to see it. By refusing to see Rome, Freud would be able to maintain his unconscious identification with Hannibal. But as Freud writes to Fliess about his Roman dreams, the city becomes associated with all frustrated or delayed ambitions. Struggling over the last drafts of his "dream book," Freud increasingly associated Rome with the unconscious he was attempting to conquer. In 1898, for example, he wrote, "I am not in a state to do anything else, except study the topography of Rome, my longing for which becomes more and more acute. The dream book is irremediably at a standstill. I lack any incentive to prepare it for publication. . . ." In 1899 he wrote, "Learning the eternal laws of life in the Eternal City would be no bad combination."[11] Only after his dream book was published did he visit Rome, and in this context one can appreciate Freud's "idle game" in *Civilization and its Discontents* of comparing Rome to the unconscious—a game that he had been playing for over thirty years.

In the dream book Freud quotes Jean Paul's question, "Which of the two . . . walked up and down his study with the greater impatience after he had formed his plan of going to Rome—Wincklemann, the Vice-Principal, or Hannibal, the Commander-in-Chief?"[12] Freud claimed that he had been inspired by Hannibal, but it was J. J. Wincklemann who was to uncover Pompei and introduce Europe to the romance of archaeology in the eighteenth century. There was more to the analogy between psychoanalysis and archaeology than decipherment, and Freud may well have been attracted to the city as a representation of the unconscious because of the overwhelming and undisputed success of archaeology in the nineteenth century. It was Schliemann and Koldewey who had produced proof of the reality of "myths" such as Troy and the Tower of Babel, and it was thus toward archaeology that Freud turned in search of metaphors for psychoanalysis. After Freud's second visit to Rome, this parallel course of the two disciplines was symbolically confirmed when he discovered that one of his fellow passengers on the voyage from Brindisi to Greece (and the Acropolis) was Wilhelm Dörpfeld, Schliemann's collaborator at Troy and a major archaeologist in his own right.

In a famous passage in *Les Fleurs du mal* Baudelaire writes, *"Fourmillante cité, cité pleine de rêves,/ Où le spectre en plein jour raccroche le passant"* [Swarming city, city full of dreams,/ Where a ghost stops a passerby in broad daylight]. T. S. Eliot cites Baudelaire in a footnote to the following passage in *The Waste Land*:

> Unreal City,
> Under the brown fog of a winter dawn,
> A crowd flowed over London Bridge, so many,
> I had not thought death had undone so many.[13]

The ghosts Eliot describes in London may draw upon Baudelaire's Parisian specter, but Eliot presses past that layer of the palimpsest to another: Dante's *Inferno*. In *The Waste Land* London is an "unreal city" where every phase of culture is accessible, from the Buddhist Sutras of India to modern advertising slogans. Like Schliemann's Troy, like Freud's Acropolis, Eliot's unconscious city registers his own wide reading and erudition, and thus his poem exhibits fragments of writing—shards of lost civilizations which his literary excavations have turned up. And like Baudelaire and Valéry, Eliot sees ancient and modern cities sharing the same desolation:

> Falling towers
> Jerusalem Athens Alexandria
> Vienna London
> Unreal

In this light, one might consider Eliot's much-discussed poetic technique as a kind of "disturbance of memory" which would include the appropriate forms of *déjà vu*, *déjà raconté*, and *fausse reconnaissance*.

Familiarity with Eliot's poem may blind us to the fact that dislocations of consciousness, such as those described by Freud and Jung, are a necessary and common determinant of artistic expression. "When that sort of thing happens to one," Jung writes,

> one cannot help taking it more seriously than something heard or read about. . . . In general, with anecdotes of that kind, one is quick to think of all sorts of explanations which dispose of the mystery. I have come to the conclusion that before we settle upon any theories in regard to the unconscious, we require many, many more experiences of it.[14]

Eliot's poetry offers little explanation for the experiences of the personal, philological, and cultural unconscious. It presents "moments in and out of time" which, like Pound's moments of insight, uncover the city's layers of significance.

In *Burnt Norton* Eliot presents a different vision of the London underground:

> Men and bits of paper, whirled by the cold wind
> That blows before and after time . . .
> .   .   .   .   .   .   .   .   .   .   .   .   .   .   .   .   .
> Time before and time after.
> Eructation of unhealthy souls
> Into the faded air.

Pound sees the Metro station as the site of natural and mythological renewal; Eliot sees the tube station as an image of the last judgment when the bodies of the dead are belched out of the earth like passengers thrown up by the Underground. In *East Coker* he describes the moment when

> an underground train, in the tube, stops too
> long between stations
> And the conversation rises and slowly fades into silence
> And you see behind every face the mental emptiness deepen
> Leaving only the growing terror of nothing to think about.

In Eliot's work the London Underground calls forth the undergrounds of classical antiquity and the Christian Middle Ages, with the first representing the cheerless eternity of pagan shades, the second the tormenting eternity of damned souls.

The moments recorded by Freud, Jung, Pound, and Eliot dramatize the ways that the city, the ultimate symbol of technological modernity, can become suddenly "unreal"—and with it our modern world. The city may thus provide a lexicon by which the unconscious expresses its skepticism about the labors of consciousness.

The leitmotif of the "Unreal City" sounds three times in *The Waste Land*, and in each instance it suggests how mind or consciousness has transformed the world into an image of itself: in "The Burial of the Dead," when the Londoners walking to work in the morning suddenly evoke the souls of the *Inferno*; in "The Fire Sermon," when "the Smyrna merchant" propositions the speaker; and in "What the Thunder Said," with its apocalyptic vision of falling towers. These are, however, more than dire occasions, signs of fatigue, and intimations that modern civilization is ready to collapse. These dangerous moments, like Freud's "disturbance of memory" and Jung's vision of a mosaic in Ravenna, also provide opportunities for reflecting on our own repressed doubts about empirical reality and the authority of reason.

But there is even more to the vision of the unconscious written across the familiar or unfamiliar streets of London or Paris, Athens or Rome, than a certain dubiousness about "reality." In "The Fire Sermon"—named after the Buddha's discourse explaining the effects of desire on the individual ego— the city appears in a context of unexpected gaiety:

> O City city, I can sometimes hear
> Beside a public bar in Lower Thames Street,
> The pleasant whining of a mandoline
> And a clatter and a chatter from within
> Where fishmen lounge at noon: where the walls
> Of Magnus Martyr hold
> Inexplicable splendour of Ionian white and gold.

This might be read simply as a scene showing how life could

be if pleasure, art, and the mysteries of divinity were harmonized. But the passage can also lead us out of London and Europe, past Rome and Athens, and even beyond Troy and Babel to India, whose sacred texts and literature have always used the city as a metaphor for all that is unreal, illusory, and transient.

In the *Lankavatara Sutra* the Buddha instructs his followers in the ways by which people become enmeshed in the nets of words: "the ignorant cling to names, signs and ideas; as their minds move along these channels they feed on multiplicities of objects and fall into the notion of an ego-soul and what belongs to it; they make discriminations of good and bad among appearances and cling to the agreeable."[15] To illustrate his argument, the Buddha alludes to the celestial musicians called the Gandharvas, whose skill in music is so great they delude people into taking illusion for truth. Linguistic discrimination, the Buddha teaches, "is like the city of the Gandharvas which the unwitting take to be a real city though it is not so in fact. The city appears as in a vision owing to their attachment to the memory of a city preserved in the mind as a seed; the city can thus be said to be existent and non-existent."

Eliot's city is quite precisely "unreal," neither real nor illusory, neither the attractive city of mandolin music nor the infernal city of the walking dead. The uncanny moments in *The Waste Land* thus are not merely infernal and apocalyptic visions of human futility; they are the few essential insights into modernity that make it possible for Eliot to conclude his poem with the lessons on selfless existence embodied in the *Brihadaranyaka Upanishad* and its fable of what the thunder said to gods, human beings, and demons.

Walter Benjamin, like Freud, Jung, Eliot, and Pound, saw the city as the central artifact of modernity calling for imagination and analysis, but he was less interested in the eternal or mythic aspects underlying it than in its historical construction and the ideology of capitalist production and consumption permeating its every stone, iron beam, rivet, and pane of glass. While Jung and Freud dreamed of Rome as guardian and archive of the unconscious, and Eliot and Pound imagined the Underground and the Metro as passageways to the deep structure of literature in myth, Benjamin concentrated, in his vast, unfinished work, *Paris: Capital of the Nineteenth Century*, on the arcades, the *passages* of Paris which conduct one from the soot and dung of the street into a labyrinthine, glass-roofed grotto where merchants display their treasures. Rather than descend, beyond the present, into a mythic realm afforded by the Tube and the Metro, Benjamin stayed at ground level, strolling through Paris and the Bibliothèque Nationale with the detached eye of a future archaeologist. The arcades, those first efforts by capital to enchant consumer products by placing them within a setting which was both magical and technologically modern, provided Benjamin with a site and a metaphor for excavating the political unconscious of the twentieth century.

In this endeavor he saw Baudelaire as predecessor and subject of his analysis. "The Paris of his poems," he writes, "is a submerged city, more submarine that subterranean. The chthonic elements of the city—its topographical formation, the old deserted bed of the Seine—doubtless left their impression on his work."[16] And on Benjamin's, whose earnest Marxist researches are permeated with an aesthete's melancholy before the weight of history. Even as Benjamin attempts to decipher what is determinedly and historically new in the culture of capitalism, the better to expose its frangibility, he exposes more devious ramifications: "It is precisely modernity that is always quoting primeval history." Much as he would like to stay on the horizontal plane of historical analysis, he is lured by sublime prospects: "in the convulsions of the commodity economy we begin to recognize the monuments of the bourgeoisie as ruins even before they have crumbled."

Modern poetry, psychoanalysis, cultural criticism, and archaeology all take fragments from the culture, the unconscious, and the underground and cast them into significant patterns. A highly focused but discrete image, a slip of the tongue, an emblematic dream, a shopwindow, a fragment of an ancient wall: properly arranged, these elements can exert an irresistible force on the mind. The same could be said of a walk through an ordinary or extraordinary city—where, quite unexpectedly, a sign, a sewer lid, or a broken clock will make one lose all sense of temporal and spatial identity with the ongoing project of modernism so evident in all cities. In such a moment, the city becomes a complex mnemonic device which undermines the palpable evidence of stone and steel: beneath one's feet and behind one's gaze another city, unconscious, ancient and modern, and included in the mythic and historical cycles of death and rebirth, suddenly comes to light.

Twenty years after writing "In a Station of the Metro," Pound discovered some striking evidence of the mythical and modern, the organic and the mechanical poles of attraction evident in a modern city and a modern poem. After explaining in his *Guide to Kulchur* that Leo Frobenius's archaeology is "immediate" rather than "retrospective," Pound casts a tantalizing piece of evidence upon the page, a single anecdote culled from Frobenius's work: "Example: the peasants opposed a railway cutting. A king had driven into the ground at that place. The engineers dug and unearthed the bronze car of Dis, two thousand years buried."[17]

**2**

# Dreaming of Egypt

All inquiry into antiquity, all curiosity respecting the Pyramids, the excavated cities, Stonehenge, the Ohio Circles, Mexico, Memphis,—is the desire to do away with this wild, savage, and preposterous There or Then, and introduce in its place the Here and the Now.

—Emerson, "History"

On the twenty-fifth of Thermidor (August 12, 1799, on the Revolutionary Calendar), Napoleon, having seized Egypt from both the Mamelukes and the suzerainty of the Ottoman Empire, entered what Egyptologists claim to be the "King's Chamber" of the Great Pyramid of Giza. Like his predecessor, Alexander the Great, he asked to be left alone in the heart of the pyramid. When he emerged he was reportedly "very pale and impressed" and forbade his aides to speak of what had happened. He later implied that he had received an intimation of his destiny, but still refused to speak of it. Even in exile at St. Helena the incident haunted him, but he would say nothing about it: "No. What's the use? You'd never believe me."[1]

But one *can* imagine what a young general embarked on world conquest in emulation of Alexander the Great might have felt inside the monumental and ancient Pyramid of the great Pharaoh Khufu (2551–2528 B.C.). Despite its reputation as a vainglorious tomb for a tyrannical Pharaoh, a legend popularized by Herodotus, there is no explicit evidence that this structure was exclusively a tomb, although that may have been one of its purposes. The Pyramids have always been admired only if they were first admitted to be evidence of a monumental egotism, "oriental" excess, and semi-barbaric fanaticism. An-

20

cient Egypt and its architectural legacy have consistently been presented as a *memento mori* to Western eyes, when they have not also appeared as a dream of sensuality and barbarism in a place and a time where extremities of all kinds merge. It should not be surprising, then, that Napoleon's revelation should be counterbalanced by more practical considerations: he had calculated that the stone contained in the Pyramids at Giza was sufficient to build a wall three meters high and one meter thick all around France. Although this calculation was simply a way of "appreciating" the enormity of the tombs (since the requisite dismantling and shipping of the stones would exceed even the engineering skills of Napoleon), it suggests extreme but related responses to the hazy reappearance of Egypt on the European horizon: romantic revery and imperial domination, metaphysical insight and technological admiration. The Egypt of the Turkish Empire could be possessed, but its antiquity, its apocalyptic vistas, were another matter. Egyptian obelisks may adorn the major cities of Europe, but "ancient Egypt" has remained in its dreams.

Consider the crowds who press through the rooms of Egyptian antiquities at the British Museum. They are not necessarily interested in archaeology, the origins of culture, or Egyptology. A solitary stroll through the magnificent collections of East Asian and Indian art the same afternoon convinces one that there must be a specific reason for this fascination with ancient Egypt. The exotic and beautiful arts of China, Siam, India, and Persia do not draw the crowds that the crude wooden sarcophagi and bundled bodies of ancient Egyptians do. To cite the obviously morbid quality of the fascination is only the beginning of an answer. For if the crowds are morbid, so apparently were the ancient Egyptians, the scholars who unearthed their bodies, and the artists who continue to dwell on their culture. Ancient Egypt would appear to be a culture where these private fascinations with death and eternity were given unabashed and monumental expression.

The idea of eternity has always been a problem for the West. The ancient Hebrews cultivated the idea that eternity could come into being only after "history" was completed, which is to say, only after the covenant of Yahweh with his people was countersigned and redeemed by the Messiah. Christ may have been the Messiah for those who followed him, but his coming did not end history, as many of the first Christians hoped. He too left the arena of human history in order to return at a later date. After the Second Coming and a thousand-year reign, then and only then could "eternity" begin. The Greeks, living in the shadow of the ancient empires of the East, distinguished themselves, like the Jews, by a specifically "historical" view of time, commemorated in the works of Herodotus and Thucydides. In the same vein, Plato could maintain his own metaphysical conceptions, which clearly drew on the legacies of the East, by inventing a realm of forms which existed outside of history. For the West, then, eternity always had to be elsewhere, at the end of Time and History or oriented within a metaphysical realm beyond ordinary human perception—whether in abstractions, mathematics, heaven, or an ever-receding future promising a technological utopia. It could never be permanently accessible here and now.

For centuries Western schoolchildren have been taught about moments of crisis, dates in our history when the bulwark of the Judeo-Christian and Greco-Roman traditions were threatened by Asia. At Marathon (490 B.C.) the Persians were stopped by the Athenians, at Poitiers (A.D. 732) the Saracens were stopped by the Franks, at Lepanto (A.D. 1573) the Turks were stopped by the Christians. At each of these crucial points, it was stressed, "Europe" might never have become what it is; it was an extremely unsettling lesson.

Despite such violent responses to the threat of Asia, Asian religions and arts have crossed over the bulwark in several waves since the romantic and industrial revolutions. The first enthusiasm followed Napoleon's conquest of Egypt and Britain's removal of its art. Hegel's philosophy, as we shall see, reflects this equivocal legacy in its attempts to both include and yet segregate the idea of Egyptian antiquity. American literature especially, as John T. Irwin has demonstrated, was taken by the figures of the hieroglyph and the pyramid. In the late nineteenth century, Japan and China were in vogue among the aesthetes and thinkers of Boston, London, and Paris. In the 1920s Howard Carter's exhumation of Tutankhamen's crypt prompted a popular sensation that influenced the movies and even the theaters where they were exhibited. In the 1960s, after more than twenty years of war against Japan, Korea, and Vietnam, a hemorrhage in the Western bulwark allowed Egyptian, Indian, Chinese, and Japanese arts and philosophies to flood the culture. In the years since the apparent collapse of the counter-culture, politicians and educators have tried to refurbish the Judeo-Christian tradition, emphasizing the uniquely liberal nature of Western societies. But those crowds at the British Museum suggest that they have failed to recognize that the attraction of the East, and Egypt in particular, is not a conscious preference for the metaphysical traditions of Asia over and above technological and historical culture. The appeal is undoubtedly unconscious, an inevitable consequence of European psychic and political imperialism.

For in a very specific sense, the mortuary art, the religious icons of Asia and Africa gathered in the British Museum, are at once imperial loot and a silent reproach to the Empire: the curiosity of the imperialist is accompanied by an identification, not with colonial peoples who were thought to be unconcerned with their archaeological treasures, but with the ancient dead. And so the funereal nature of Egyptian art and culture seems to allegorize its own future antiquity—and that of Britain. It is precisely in this way that the American poet Hilda Doolittle (H. D.), in *The Walls Do Not Fall*, writes of the London blitz and of ancient Egypt. Bearing the dedication "for Karnak 1923 / from London 1942," this reflection on personal and cultural memory presents the ruins of the British Empire in the idiom of antiquity:

> mist and mist-grey, no colour,
> still the Luxor bee, chick and hare
> pursue unalterable purpose
>
> in green, rose-red, lapis;
> they continue to prophesy
> from the stone papyrus:

> there, as here, ruin opens
> the tomb, the temple; enter,
> there as here, there are no doors:
>
> the shrine lies open to the sky,
> the rain falls, here, there
> sand drifts; eternity endures.[2]

If we are to understand the particular lure of ancient Egypt, we will have to distinguish it from other features of Orientalism: imaginary places like Babylon, Araby, India, and Cathay. When one reads of Egypt in the book of Genesis it evokes little awe or wonder. For Joseph and the Israelites who fall under its yoke, Egypt is little more than a granary and a prison. "Egypt," for those who were able to know it at least in the twilight of its power, had yet to be seen in the splendid desolation it presented to the Greeks. When Herodotus visited Egypt in the fifth century before Christ, it was a Persian satrapy whose greatest glories had to be imagined. It is impossible, then, to appreciate what ancient Egypt is without recognizing that it has always been an artifact of Western desires. Since it had already passed from the stage of world history when it entered Western consciousness, ancient Egypt would forever retain the allure of incomprehensible mysteries associated with the time before one's birth. Its fascination could never have been anything but an internal threat to the West's sense of self-sufficiency and superiority.

It was in this way that Shelley imagined one of Egypt's greatest Pharaohs, Ramses II, otherwise known as Ozymandias:

> Two vast and trunkless legs of stone
> Stand in the desert . . . Near them, on the sand,
> Half sunk, a shattered visage lies, whose frown,
> And wrinkled lip, and sneer of cold command,
> Tell that its sculptor well those passions read
> Which yet survive, stamped on those lifeless things.[3]

The sculptor who "read" the passions of Ozymandias in his frown and lip was no less distant from the Pharaoh than "the traveller from an antique land" whose words Shelley pretends to quote. The embodiment of upper and lower Egypt, the divine King's passions can only be inferred from the writing on his face which the sculptor transcribes on "those lifeless things" which the traveler encounters fallen in the sand. Whether one approaches its pyramids, its art, or its writing, "Egypt," unlike India or China, implies a kind of irreducible distance, both in time and in space, which suggests death or eternity. Despite its spatial coincidence with modern Egypt, this "Egypt" is a different country entirely.

The deciphering of the Egyptian hieroglyphics was thus of more than philological interest in the Napoleonic era and after. Indeed, since the time of the neoplatonists, hieroglyphics were regarded as a magical picture-writing which probably concealed secrets long lost to the world. This tradition engendered the idea that the hieroglyphs must be deciphered as pictographs or *aides mémoire*. The opposing rational approach emphasized the idea that the script was phonetic and must be approached as an alphabetic language. Despite the Rosetta stone's original promise as a key to the writing (containing as it did a single message written in hieroglyphics, Coptic, and Greek), the secret of the hieroglyphs remained secure until the French linguistic genius Jean-François Champollion, who had prepared since he was a child for the task, produced the rudiments of a hieroglyphic grammar. Champollion recognized that the script was neither exclusively pictographic nor alphabetic; it contained elements of both. The excitement following Champollion's discovery is not difficult to understand, but the particularly "Egyptian" quality of the fascination can be better appreciated in its contrast to another, more impressive act of deciphering. Georg Grotefend's decipherment of cuneiform, the wedge-writing of Mesopotamia, was achieved without the equivalent of the Rosetta stone. Yet this astounding achievement brought him little notoriety and generated little interest in cuneiform. Hieroglyphics had a strangely popular hold on the European imagination, perhaps because they could be understood, not as words, but as images of a living world no longer alive, a world of hawks, hares, eyes, men, women, and serpents. They seemed oddly familiar but entirely alien, almost like the sensations of *déjà vu* brought on by the correspondence between a waking vision and a forgotten dream—of a lost world wherein living things, rather than abstract marks, were not only significant, but vocal and eloquent.

In Hegel's dealings with Egypt one sees an influential example of a typical Western ambivalence. He is obviously moved by Egypt and its propensity for evoking sublime response:

> Besides the other lands already enumerated as belonging to the Persian Empire, Egypt claims notice—characteristically the Land of Ruins; a land which from hoary antiquity has been regarded with wonder, and which in recent times also has attracted the greatest interest. Its ruins, the final result of immense labor, surpass in the gigantic and monstrous all that antiquity has left us.[4]

But he is no less insistent about its limitations: "The Sphinx may be regarded as a symbol of the Egyptian Spirit. The human head looking out from the brute body exhibits Spirit as it begins to emerge from the merely Natural." Hegel's analysis returns again and again to the contradictory aspects of Egypt: its language, which is both phonetic and pictographic; its art, which is both accomplished and rude; its geography, poised between a "stupid" African element and "Oriental massiveness," and its history, in which the "Mythical is blended with the Historical."

Hegel's recurrent rebukes to those, like Leibniz, who claimed the superiority of pictographic to alphabetic scripts reveals his own mixture of attraction and disdain for the idea of Egypt. In Egyptian art, "The brute form is . . . turned into a symbol: it is also partly degraded to a mere hieroglyphic sign." Egyptian brutishness both offends and entices: it is able to imagine the symbolic and spiritual, which Hegel values, only by inventing hieroglyphs, which are naively mimetic and external, composed of hawks, hares, hands, eyes, and pyramids. Egyptians, according to Hegel, could not "think" internally—only outwardly through writing and architecture:

> it has no other material or ground to work on, in order to teach itself what it is—to realize itself for itself—than this working out

its thoughts in stone; and what it engraves on the stone are its
enigmas—these hieroglyphs. They are of two kinds—hieroglyphs *proper*, designed rather to express language, and having
reference to subjective conception; and a class of hieroglyphs
of a different kind, viz. those enormous masses of architecture
and sculpture with which Egypt is covered.

Egypt is thus a vast writing surface upon which these "hieroglyphs" are inscribed as an expression of its spiritual struggles
toward a European or Greek notion of the Spirit. The ruins of
these hieroglyphs "are greater and more worthy of astonishment than all other works of ancient or modern time."

One could expect that Hegel's ongoing argument against
hieroglyphic writing in *The Philosophy of Mind* (the Third Book
of his *Encyclopedia*) would register, if only at the level of metaphor, ambivalence about the Egyptian legacy. Distinguishing
between the "Sign," whose meaning is conventionalized and
hence arbitrary, and the "Symbol," whose meaning derives
from its representation of a visible object, Hegel writes, "The
sign is some immediate intuition, representing a totally different import from what naturally belongs to it; it is the pyramid into which a foreign soul has been conveyed, and where
it is conserved."[5] Even while arguing for the superiority of
alphabetic (and European) culture over hieroglyphic (and
Asian) culture, Hegel is drawn to link the sign, and thus the
alphabetic letter, with the Egyptian symbol par excellence, the
pyramid.

Jacques Derrida has provided a thorough analysis of these
contradictions which concludes by arguing that Hegelian Idealism, like the Great Pyramid, guards an enigma: "Intelligence
keeps these images in reserve, submerged at the bottom of a
very dark shelter, like the water in a nightlike or unconscious
pit . . . or rather like a precious vein at the bottom of the mine."[6]
The vast edifice of Hegelian—of European—idealism rests upon
and guards its inutterable (primitive, brutish, "African") other.
One can appreciate the power of this enigmatic interplay of
corporeal and spiritual, hieroglyphic and alphabetic, Asian and
European values in Hegel's strange remarks about "those Wonders of the World, the Pyramids, whose destination, though

stated long ago by Herodotus and Diodorus, has been only recently expressly confirmed—to the effect, viz., that these prodigious crystals with their geometrical regularity contain dead bodies." The Pyramids of Giza contained no such bodies in Hegel's time; in fact there is still no firm evidence that they ever did. Although some remains have been found in pyramid fields to the south, the Pyramids had only begun to be examined by Europeans when Hegel wrote. Hegel's insistence that the purpose of these massive structures had been finally determined cannot but register a certain anxiety about their purpose: what if the advancement of the spirit which his philosophic works describe, beginning in brute material consciousness and rising toward Absolute Knowledge, concealed at its origin something more than the barbaric, the unselfconscious "monstrosities" of Pharaonic egotism? What if these monuments signify a sophistication which would substantiate the smiling condescension of the Egyptian priests who told Herodotus that the Greeks were but children? This is a doubt that Hegel cannot allow himself to utter.

The most recent stage in the idealizing of writing can be found in the "Writing Room" of the British Museum: there one can pick up, free of charge, a four-page pamphlet entitled "The Story of Writing" by Albertine Gaur. Without much preparation the visitor is taken from pictographic characters and Gothic calligraphy to this definition of writing:

> The purpose of writing is information storage. Each society stores the information essential to its economic and political continuation. . . . The need for a systematic form of writing is in many ways closely connected with the idea of property, its protection (state), exchange (trade), and administration (government). Trade and administration rather than religion and literature have been the foster-parents of literacy.[7]

Like Hegel, Gaur wants to remove the origin and the purpose of writing from any figural or imaginative context. Where Hegel sees the Spirit embroiled in unreflected nature, Gaur sees primitive people struggling on the road to the Information Age: writing stores information in the same way that magnetic tape stores the digital translations of natural language. In both cases, the rude and brutish, the smelly qualities of the world, are lost in the ascent toward Spirit and property. When she approaches Egyptian writing, Gaur is attentive only to the ways in which ideograms and determinatives are combined:

> When writing a word the Egyptian scribe could choose between various methods. He could for example simply write the appropriate ideogram followed by a vertical stroke:

p-r (house)

More frequently he could use single consonant signs followed by a determinative:

w-b-n (rise/shine on)

=w    =b    =n    ⊙ =determinative (sun)

Or he could use a double consonant sign, followed by two single consonant signs, repeating two consonants already expressed by the double consonant sign, followed by a determinative.

m-r (pyramid)

m-r    =m    =r    =determinative (pyramid)

Hieroglyphic writing is understood technically as an early approach to an alphabetic script. When Gaur turns to the advantages of alphabetic writing, one learns that "writing thus becomes more economic, less labour-intensive in relation to the time required to learn how to read and write, and information can be stored in less space. Phonetic scripts are altogether more cost-effective." Hegel and Gaur read hieroglyphics as an inferior or developing script, which at best could advance toward, respectively, Spirit and Information. And both, quite intentionally, base their analyses on a refutation of the figurative and imaginary element. One could say that they actively repress this element of writing, like an embarrassing or bad dream.

When Freud chose a metaphor to illustrate the nature of the dream, he turned to the hieroglyph—for here was the very type of the enigma. To dream, Freud claimed, was to engage in a

kind of psychic picture-writing. Freud interpreted dreams neither as code, such as one finds in the ancient Greek *Oneirok-
ritikon* which provided a rote lexicon of dream images and their
meanings, nor as the bearers of symbolic or allegorical interpretations one finds in myth and literature. Instead he insisted
that dreams be understood to contain elements of a personal
and idiosyncratic kind of "writing" which our sleeping minds
produce in order both to express the unconscious and to repress
it. In making this distinction, Freud followed, perhaps without
knowing it, Charles Baudelaire's division between "natural" and
"absurd" or "hieroglyphic"[8] dreams. "The productions of the
dream-work," Freud writes, "present no greater difficulties to
their translators than do the ancient hieroglyphic scripts to those
who seek to read them."[9] Modesty prevents him from pointing
out that "translators" of both scripts had to await someone gifted
enough to break their codes. But whereas Champollion's grammar and lexicon could be learned by patient scholars, Freud's
dream grammar required the "peculiar gifts" which characterize
"artistic activity."

However intellectual and laborious the measures taken,
both Champollion and Freud were superbly "gifted" by nature
with abilities that cannot be taught by Egyptological and psy-
choanalytic grammars. Recognizing this, Freud admits that an
earlier and perhaps more powerful precedent for his discovery
was Joseph, who interpreted the dream of the Pharaoh and so
saved Egypt from famine. "It will be noticed," he writes in a
footnote, "that the name of Joseph plays a great part in my
dreams. . . . My own ego finds it very easy to hide itself behind
people of that name, since Joseph was the name of a man
famous in the Bible as an interpreter of dreams." And here one
sees the relationship between Egypt and dreams deepen.

Joseph was not only the favorite of Jacob, he was a great
dreamer:

> And Joseph dreamed a dream, and he told it to his brethren,
> and they hated him yet the more. And he said unto them, Hear,
> I pray you, this dream which I have dreamed: For behold, we
> were binding sheaves in the field and, lo, my sheaf arose, and
> also stood upright; and, behold, your sheaves stood round
> about, and made obeisance to my sheaf.　(Gen. 37.5–7)

To avenge themselves on their father's favorite, the brothers sell Joseph into Egyptian slavery. But as in a dream, opposites reverse themselves, and their betrayal leads to the realization of Joseph's prophetic dream. He becomes vizier of Egypt by interpreting the Pharaoh's dreams as prophecies of the coming years of plenty and famine. Joseph's prophetic dreams are realized through the interpretation of dreams: he realizes his dreams by delving into them and finding their meanings in God's will. "Do not interpretations belong to God?" (40.8), he asks the imprisoned butler and baker who learn of his gift.

In this context of dreams, gifts, and prophecies, one can appreciate the ironies of a letter Freud wrote to Fliess in 1900 after the publication of *The Interpretation of Dreams*: "Do you suppose," he writes, "that some day a marble tablet will be placed on this house, inscribed with these words?—

> In This House on July 24th, 1895
> the Secret of Dreams was Revealed
> to Dr. Sigm. Freud

At the moment there seems little prospect of it." Much more than this has been accorded Freud, but it began with a disciplined gift which echoed Joseph's favor with God. He learned to read the ancient script which is repeated every night in our dreams, a script neither strictly phonetic nor pictographic, neither symbolic nor coded by a simple key, neither rational nor irrational, neither "ours" nor an "other's." In dreams, Freud discovered that ancient Egypt carried on its existence in the interplay of the unconscious realm of desires and drives and the conscious arbitration of our acquired faculties of repression. Writing in the twilight of the imperial era, Freud describes the return of the repressed in the return of ancient scripts, primitive representations, non-European myths and narratives, unconscious expressions—all characteristics of artistic modernism.

Twenty years after what Freud called his "Egyptian Dream Book" was published, Howard Carter began to uncover the greatest of all archaeological treasures, the untouched burial vaults of Tutankhamen. The discoveries prompted near hysteria in the newspapers and tabloids. The death of Carter's sponsor, the Earl of Carnarvon, and of others involved in the dig in subsequent years inspired the legend of Tutankhamen's curse against those who interrupted his astral existence in the Western Lands by breaking into his sarcophagus. The curse had no foundation in the actual messages deciphered in the burial chambers, but it accurately reflected a popular prejudice against the desecration of the vaults of Pharaohs and, by inference, the unconscious desire for "eternity." The popular themes are as simple as they are universal: vengeance awaits those who would tamper with the silent chambers of the dead, even in the name of Science. Even as the papers clamored for more sensational finds than archaeological science had made, they encouraged the notion that science's work was improper and unholy, even dangerous.

A fitting expression of these ambiguous responses appeared in the movies and in the palaces which exhibited them. In Hollywood especially, the first theaters were monumental and grandiose halls styled in various exotic vocabularies. Grauman's Chinese, the Egyptian, and the Vista Theatre were designed to overwhelm moviegoers with sensational effects. A customer walking into the Vista from Sunset Boulevard entered an exotic and arcane hall where forbidding priestly heads stared from the walls. Like an initiate, the viewer passed a series of forbidding icons before admission to the mysteries—and these were nothing less than a spectral show of images flickering upon a screen. This most advanced form of mechanical reproduction required the most archaic atmosphere to have the maximum effect.

Like a series of hieroglyphs on a papyrus, the figures and scenes unrolled from revolving reels concealed in the projectionist's booth. Sergei Eisenstein referred to "the new language of Cinema" as one which could reach audiences in ways more profound than theatrical or literary narratives. It was as if moviemakers were inducting the masses into a secret order characterized by a private language. By employing montage, which juxtaposes significant images to advance the plot and to make dramatic points, the filmmakers were drawing on the logic of hieroglyphics and dreams. According to Eisenstein, film was founded on the "copulation (perhaps we had better say, the combination) of two hieroglyphs" and thus could not be understood according to the "inflexible *letter of the alphabet*."[10] For this reason, René Clair described movies as a "writing in images" which replicated the interrelationship of pictographic and phonetic notation: "In the cinema all we have is the image. The printed intertitles are a frigid commentary."[11] The audience was induced to forget its phonetic and literary senses of narrative and to learn unconsciously a new script based on what Clair called "cinematic syntax": juxtaposed images, montage, close-ups, jump-cuts, flashbacks, and foreshadowings. Eisenstein referred to this "visual overtone" resulting from montage to "an actual piece, an actual element of—a fourth dimension!" The movie screen, like the painted walls on an Egyptian tomb, like the dreams inside our brains, presents a metaphysical space where time no longer operates according to its ordinary, relentless logic. All of these forms of expression actually "projected" the soul, the desires, and the shadows of life into a beyond. It was universally and unaccountably intoxicating.

The unconscious had found, with the help of technology, a public forum veiled in various exotic styles. For several hours, a moviegoer could escape the pressurized and competitive culture of modernity. It is not difficult to appreciate the enormous worldwide popularity of a series of "horror" films produced by Universal Pictures in the early thirties. *Frankenstein, Dracula,* and *The Mummy* dramatize the punishment awaiting those who do not understand the limits of science.

In *The Mummy* (1932, directed by Karl Freund), the theme emerges through a conflict between the archaeological rigor of an experienced Egyptologist and the understandable curiosity of a young scholar who reads a hieroglyphic spell that revives the mummy of one Imhotep (Boris Karloff) buried alive 3,700 years before. Reading the spell frees the mummy from his bandages, and appropriately enough the young man replaces the ancient Egyptian by losing his sanity and dying in a straitjacket. Imhotep's crime was to have loved and attempted to revive the virgin Princess Ankh-es-an-amon, whose soul had found refuge in the body of Helen Grosvenor, a beautiful young lady, half-British and half-Egyptian, living in Cairo. The audience first sees her gazing out a window at the Great Pyramid of Giza, while behind her a party of elegant Europeans dance and chat in luxurious and exotic rooms. Dreaming of ancient Egypt in the midst of this rich imperial scene, Helen represents the contradiction between the material benefits of modernism funded by colonialism and the spiritual desires the East has at times awakened in the European marauder. Being both British and Egyptian, she can chastise a young archaeologist at the party for his callous exhumation of the princess even while falling in love with him.

At the same time, memories of her former existence are summoned when Imhotep prays at the Cairo Museum over the mummy of the princess. Drawn to Imhotep's villa, she is shown on the surface of a pool a waking dream which becomes the screen onto which the film-projector and the audience cast their own imagery. The dream-film tells how her ancient lover attempted to revive her with the hieroglyphic spell and how he was buried alive for his pains. She is thus influenced by two loves, one unconscious and Egyptian and the other conscious and British. In anguish, her young lover exclaims: "Three thousand seven hundred years ago—what has that got to do with us today?" The movie demonstrates how very much antiquity has to do with the present, because Helen's dilemma focuses the contradictions implicit in the appeal of a movie called *The Mummy* shown in a modern theater made to resemble an Egyptian tomb. It was as if cinema, dreaming, and writing all shared the fundamental, the esoteric, elements of the same technology.

Derrida would call these apparently disparate media instances of a generalized "writing," which is to say everything that "gives rise to an inscription in general, whether it is literal or not and even if what it distributes in space is alien to the order of the voice."[12] One could then include "Egypt" within this definition of writing, especially since it has been subject to the same forms of repression.

Derrida's analysis of the Western repression of writing begins by noting that ethnocentrism has always "controlled the concept of writing." We can readily see the truth of this observation. Hegel believes hieroglyphics to be a mute and unselfconscious writing struggling from its Oriental and African origins toward Greek and alphabetic ideality. Freud uses hieroglyphics to describe the dream-work that results from the repression of the unconscious, suggesting that individual psyches and world history have similar foundations. Gaur regards hieroglyphics as a less than "cost-effective" method of inscription surpassed by alphabetic "information storage" and seeks to refute the common notion that it arose as a response to mythology and religion. In each case, hieroglyphic writing is something which must be overcome, transcended, or repressed because of its supposedly naive imitation of the visible world. Since Egyptian religion prefigures Western notions of immortality, the soul, and the dying God (Osiris/Christ), it has entered into European reflection as a dangerous yet enticing version of metaphysical values. The problem with Egyptian metaphysics has generally been considered its inability to sufficiently distinguish between material and spiritual existence, plurality and unity, images and ideas. Tempted as he is by the proximity of Egyptian and Western values, the popular Egyptologist Wallis Budge sums up the European response:

> The Egyptians, being fundamentally an African people, possessed all the virtues and vices which characterized the North African races generally, and it is not to be held for a moment that any African people could ever become metaphysicians in the modern sense of the word. In the first place, no African language is suitable . . . to theological and philosophical speculations, and even an Egyptian priest of the highest intellectual attainments would have been unable to render a treatise of Aristotle into language which his brother priests without teaching could understand. The mere construction of the language would make such a thing an impossibility, to say nothing of the ideas of the great Greek philosopher, which belong to a domain of thought and culture wholly foreign to the Egyptian.[13]

Budge, Hegel, and other Westerners dreaming of Egypt were threatened into condemning precisely those aspects of Egypt which they admired the most: the figural, the plural, the sub-lime, a metaphysics unchanneled by the logic of concepts and the law of noncontradiction. Hieroglyphic language threatened European notions of property, as Derrida writes in *Glas*, because "the first language properly so called is . . . 'double (*zweideutig*),' enigmatic; it brings into play the contraries between the conscious and the unconscious, on two scenes at once."[14] Logocentric culture has refused the fascination with Egypt felt by Hegel, Budge, and others all but a critical and condescending expression.

But this considered condemnation was accompanied by a nearly equal and opposite, however ignorant, infatuation with the "idea" of "Egypt" which led to what Derrida calls "a *hieroglyphic prejudice*."[15] "The occultation, far from proceeding, as it would seem, from ethnocentric scorn, takes the form of an hyperbolic admiration" in the works of Athanasius Kircher and others who blindly assumed that hieroglyphics concealed a truly metaphysical knowledge of the ultimate mysteries of human beings and their history. In the same way, Friedrich Schlegel would speak of Sanskrit not only as an ancient heir of the European languages, but as the remnant of a divine speech. The effect of this mystical infatuation was to further encourage the rational denunciation of Egypt and its writing: each attempt to understand Egyptian culture outside the confines of Western rationalism could be checked by sober charges of "exoticism." There thus emerged, as Derrida writes, "a certain complicity" "between rationalism and mysticism."

Michel Serres has described a pivotal moment in this Western internalization of Egypt by elaborating on a fabulous narrative of Thales' visit to Giza. Seeing that the Pyramid acted as a monumental gnomon which transformed the surrounding desert from mere earth into a sundial, Thales reputedly reversed this function in order to determine not the time of day, but the height of the Pyramid: "Instead of letting the pyramid speak of the sun, or the constant determine the scale of the variable, he asks the sun to speak of the pyramid; that is, he asks the object in motion to provide a constant flow of information about the object at rest."[16] Thales does this by measuring the shadow of the Pyramid at the precise moment that his own shadow is equal to his height. Serres makes of this story the archetypal instance in which Greek rationality is revealed as a ruse designed to elicit knowledge of the distant, the vast, and the unscalable through the interposition of a model: thus the invention of Greek geometry: "His mathematics is the relation between shadows, two secrets, two forms and two ciphers, relation or logos, relationship and utterance to be transmitted, utterance which transmits a relationship. . . . The sand on which the sun leaves its trace is a screen, the wall at the back of the cave." And so the sciences of geometry, of rationalism, of anthropology (if one recognizes that Thales' response to the Great Pyramid is one of the first attempts by the West to measure or size up the East) are in effect a science of shadows. Coming presumably to learn from Egypt, Thales is remembered for having measured its principal monument. Like Napoleon's two thousand years later, Thales' astonishment is quickly overcome by calculation.

Indeed, the fundamental Western reaction to Egypt can be summarized by its assumptions about the Great Pyramid. For Herodotus, as for Hegel, the Pyramid is a cause for wonder. "What most excites our wonder at first sight of these astonishing constructions," Hegel writes, "is their extraordinary magnitude, which at once makes us reflect upon the duration of time, the variety, superabundance and persistence of human energies which is inseparable from the completion of such colossal buildings."[17] This wonder is both tempered and increased by the assumption that this monument was "just" a tomb. Herodotus reports that Khufu was, more than two thousands years after his death, still reviled for this display of egotism. Khufu, Herodotus reports, "brought the country into all sorts of misery. He closed all the temples, then, not content with excluding his subjects from the practice of their religion, compelled them without exception to labour as slaves for his own advantage."[18] The astonishment which the Pyramids evoke is both diminished and increased by this assumption that they were built strictly for personal glory. There is indeed a certain complicity between fascination and condemnation in this astonished gaze. "Despite all the wonder they arouse of their own accord," Hegel writes, "[they] are nothing but crystals, mere shells, which enclose a kernel, that is, a departed spirit, and serve as custodians of this still consistent bodily presence and form."[19] One sees in both cases the way in which a moralistic Western judgment is invoked to reduce the undeniably overwhelming effects of the Pyramids—and of Egypt, of which they are the most powerful emblem.

The Egyptologist Ahmed Fakhry claims that the classical legends of Khufu's tyranny are unfounded: "Ancient Egyptian history provides no evidence at all to support these stories. Khufu was apparently an able and energetic ruler, during whose reign the land flourished and art reached perfection."[20] Fakhry nevertheless maintains the idea that the Pyramids are "just" tombs: "Archeological research has proved beyond doubt that the Great Pyramid is nothing more or less than a tomb for King Khufu." Fakhry's scholarly intentions notwithstanding, his standard history of the Pyramids *proves*, by any rigorous scientific standards, nothing of the kind, as any mildly curious perusal of his evidence will show. It is perhaps likely that pyramids are tombs. That they are only tombs seems unlikely. And in any case, Egyptologists seem less than curious about the meaning of the pyramid as an architectural form and the significance of entombment. Considering the fact that the Pharaoh was a living god and the embodiment of the nation and its people, modern notions of burial seem inadequate to comprehend its political and metaphysical meaning.

Peter Tompkins explains that for centuries

> It was attributed to chance that the foundations [of the Great Pyramid] were almost perfectly oriented to true north, that its structure incorporated a value for pi (the constant by which the diameter of a circle may be multiplied to give its true circumference) accurate to several decimals and in several distinct and unmistakable ways; that its main chamber incorporated the "sacred" 3-4-5 and $2\text{-}\sqrt{5}\text{-}3$ triangles ($a^2 + b^2 = c^2$) which were to make Pythagoras famous, and which Plato in his *Timaeus* claimed as the building blocks of the cosmos.[21]

Tompkins asserts that "an advanced science did flourish in the

Middle East at least three thousand years before Christ, and that Pythagoras, Eratosthenes, Hipparchus and other Greeks reputed to have originated mathematics on this planet merely picked up fragments of an ancient science evolved by remote and unknown predecessors." Even to make such learned and unpretentious observations as Tompkins does invite charges of pseudo-scholarship and romantic fancy. What is behind this immediate distrust but the fear that Greece was but a narrow, rough entrance into the West, the censor for a knowledge considered even now to be semi-civilized, foreign, dream-like?

If Egypt in general and the Pyramids in particular have had such powerful effects, it is because they have allowed the unconscious to speak—in boundless feeling, in uncanniness, in an expansive selflessness. For fewer places on earth could appear so substantially in space, so resistant to the effects of time. "Man fears Time, but Time fears the Pyramid," the light show staged at Giza announces. If this is true it is because the Pyramid has acted as a vast mnemonic device, recalling to people a certain unconscious skepticism about the reality of Time. Archeologists, Theosophists, Freemasons, Rosicrucians, and contemporary sects of the New Age have claimed the Great Pyramid to be a vast tomb, a chamber for the elevation of adepts, an astronomical observatory, an archive of lost sciences, a prophecy in stone, a hall of weights and measures. Those interested in its purely physical properties have argued that it conducts energy, slows organic decay, and even sharpens the edges of razors. Its enormous mass, its portentous geometrical perfection, its precise orientation to the cardinal points of the compass, its antiquity: all of these persuade its enthusiasts that it commemorates, prognosticates, describes, conceals, or measures things of great interest to our age.

Freud might have explained these metaphysical interests in terms of the unconscious death drive. In *Beyond the Pleasure Principle* he claims that we are driven "to reach an ancient goal by paths alike old and new. . . . If we are to take it as a truth that knows no exception that everything living dies for *internal reasons*—becomes inorganic once again—then we shall be compelled to say that *the aim of all life is death.*"[22] The "ancient goal" we seek, Freud claims, is equilibrium of the sort associated with death and displayed at Giza, at the Valley of the Kings, at the Temples at Karnak, or encrypted within our dreams. We also find this "ancient goal" in the unsettling familiarity of hieroglyphs, in the effect produced by reading difficult texts which we only partially understand, and at times in the movie theater when we are seized by emotions the movies have not in themselves produced.

Pyramidologists have supposed that the Great Pyramid, despite the thousands of years that have elapsed since Herodotus first described it in his *Histories*, still hides undiscovered chambers. The idea is that certain sound waves, caused by the recitation of a chant or mantra would open the chamber. Precisely in this way, the unconscious vaults are opened by certain words, images, or echoes which have correspondences in the unconscious. In their book on Freud's "Wolf Man," Nicolas Abraham and Maria Torok refer to "cryptonyms," words which have "encrypted" other words in order to repress a nearly ultimate, "taboo word" which would open the unconscious like a magic word opens a secret vault.[23] Where Abraham and Torok see the unconscious as a crypt of the unspeakable, Julian Jaynes regards crypts and pyramids as "mansions for voices," archives wherein the hallucinated voices of the divine kings are conserved in hieroglyphics.[24] Whether they are the tomb of the unspeakable or the reserve of voices which never cease, the Pyramids can never be finally and completely robbed of their contents. Indeed, Freud compared the tensions between conscious forgetting and unconscious memory to the "manner in which tourists are conducted to the top of the Great Pyramid of Giza by being pushed from one direction and pulled from the other."[25] The unconscious remains, like the Great Pyramid, the archive of the unsaid and the unthought—the historical point of contact with the eternal world.

These irresolvable tensions constitute the very fabric of language, as Derrida explains in his essay on *"différance."* Describing the equivocal nature of the unvoiced "a" which permits both the senses of "deferring" and "differing" in this key word that both names and mimics the way language functions, he writes,

> Now it happens, I would say in effect, that this graphic difference (*a* instead of *e*), this marked difference between two apparently vocal notations, between two vowels, remains purely graphic: it is read, or it is written, but it cannot be heard. It cannot be apprehended in speech, and we will see why it also bypasses the order of apprehension in general. It is offered by a mute mark, by a tacit monument, I would even say by a pyramid, thinking not only of the form of the letter when it is printed as a capital, but also of the text in Hegel's *Encyclopedia* in which the body of the sign is compared to the Egyptian Pyramid.[26]

Where Hegel sees the letter as a pyramid into which a foreign body has been laid, Derrida sees instead that a pyramid is nested within the letter, just as the Egyptians nested one sarcophagus within another. And not just any letter: the first letter: A.

Throughout this essay I have spoken of the relationship between Egypt and something I have called the "eternal." It is not a word with much critical or theoretical standing, mainly because few care to recognize the difference between the infinitely long and the timeless. To dream of Egypt, as I believe Westerners have since the collapse of the metaphysical order of Catholicism and the advent of scientific and liberal culture, is not very different from the appreciation of the sublime: it is a response to distances, abysses, dangers, and self-annihilation. It is a kind of ecstasy.

In this light one may reconsider what Napoleon and others have read in this cryptic legend written across the stones and columns of Egypt. Napoleon in the King's Chamber of the Great Pyramid entered for a moment into the mystery of a space which vaporizes our notion that eternity awaits the end of our lives, the completion of history, and the culmination of time. If Napoleon saw his own future as the first Emperor of France, he also saw Waterloo, Elba, St. Helena, and the "ancient goal" of his ambition, which is death. Perhaps a future emperor following Alexander into the Great Pyramid of Giza could think of little else.

# 3

## Inmost India

Pour l'enfant, amoureux de cartes et d'estampes,
L'univers est égal à son vaste appetit.
Ah! que le monde est grand à la clarté des lampes!
Aux yeux du souvenir que le monde est petit.
—Baudelaire, "Le Voyage"

We probably never overcome our first impressions of distant countries, however much we may later learn of them through books and personal experience. For most of us this means that the colors, conventions, and legends of maps continue to exert their influences long after we have overlayed them with different names, boundaries, and associations. For most Westerners, India is, in essence, a tea-yellow country, marked with vein-like rivers the color of ink, reaching into the Indian Ocean, which is aquamarine. There it seems to whirl, like a dancer, on the edge of a flagstone the shape of Ceylon. And yet this cartographic vision carries with it the color of another skin, the horizon at sea, and the promise of a final and irrevocable revelation.

In 1783 the jurist and linguist Sir William Jones embarked on a journey to the very point on European maps which represented the idea or the possibility of access to a *beyond*: wisdom, riches, sensuality, and spirit all shimmering like a mirage. He sailed from Portsmouth for Calcutta and his appointment to the High Court of Bengal with a confirmed sense of European superiority. And yet he was also seemingly ready to be seduced by the exotic and alien worlds which maps tend to create.

Already the master of the ancient and modern languages of

Europe, as well as Arabic and Persian, Jones had no expectation that he would be able to add Sanskrit to his achievements, nor did he acquire this knowledge for some time after establishing himself and his wife in India. But in his opening remarks to the Asiatick Society in Calcutta he described an event which, in retrospect, revealed what was clearly a vocation:

> When I was at sea last August, on my voyage to this country, which I had long and ardently desired to visit, I found one evening, on inspecting the observations of the day, that *India* lay before us, and *Persia* on our left, whilst a breeze from *Arabia* blew nearly on our stern. . . . It gave me inexpressible pleasure to find myself in the midst of so noble an amphitheater, almost encircled by the vast regions of *Asia*.[1]

The ineffable, the theatrical, the vast: Asia appears to Jones as an ancient promise of revelation, strangely alive, even in the age of Reason.

India, the idea of India at least, allowed Jones the opportunity to elude the overwhelming effects, and overcome the debilitating influences, of classical Mediterranean culture. Beyond the inner sea and the Atlantic Ocean, beyond the Arabian Sea and the Indian Ocean, lay an unknown world which could truly claim to be both ancient and modern, even "classical." After his vision on board ship of the "vast regions of Asia," Jones could only journey forward into what Coleridge would call "inmost Ind"—into the dawn-like distances where ancient languages and wisdoms persisted, under Western eyes, amid squalor. It must have been the fulfillment of a European classicist's secret wish: to speak an ancient language as a contemporary, to join the advantages of modernity and antiquity, to penetrate mysteries veiled even to the ancients. Later Jones would exult: "I converse fluently in *Arabick* with the Maulavi's, in *Sanscrit* with the Pandit's, and in *Persian* with the nobles of the country; thus possessing an advantage, which neither Pythagoras nor Solon possessed, though they must ardently have wished it."[2]

And yet Jones would only take up the study of Sanskrit some two years after debarking and then only because he distrusted the Pandits who dispensed translations of Hindu law for a price. Ever the vigilant sahib, Jones could plunder what he called the "mine of Sanskrit" only because he saw certain imperial benefits in it. Jones explained that the Laws of Manu needed to be translated because they were "actually revered as the word of the Most High" and that an orderly Hindu populace "would add largely to the wealth of *Britain*." And yet the preliminary philological task of dating this particular mining operation, where Sanskrit and wealth are found in the same veins, proved a baffling one. "We are lost in an inextricable labyrinth of imaginary astronomical cycles, *Yugas*, *Mahayugas*, *Calpas*, and *Menwantaras*, in attempting to calculate the time, when the first Menu, according to the *Brahmens*, governed this world."[3] However dismayed by this labyrinth, Jones would happily wander into this timeless world. For a European intellectual whose world could be accurately dated to a mere 5,787 years, there must have been something liberating about such nearly infinite chronological cycles. Less than two hundred years later, Westerners would inhabit, following the discovery of the expanding universe, something akin to this fabulous Indian temporality: the universe is now thought to be about twenty billion years old, and that perhaps but the latest in a cycle of created and destroyed worlds.

Not long after his studies in Sanskrit began, Jones felt confident in announcing to the Asiatick Society of Bengal the most startling conclusion offered in the history of linguistics:

> The Sanskrit language, whatever be its antiquity, is of a wonderful structure: more perfect than the *Greek*, more copious than the *Latin*, and more exquisitely refined than either, yet bearing to both of them a stronger affinity, both in the roots of verbs and in the forms of grammar, than could possibly have been produced by accident; so strong, indeed, that no philologer could examine them all three, without believing them to have sprung from some common source, which, perhaps, no longer exists.[4]

In one stroke, Jones breached Europe's noble and arrogant isolation from the world. More "perfect" than the Greek and more "copious" than Latin—this is remarkable, shattering praise to render to a pagan tongue, and one suspects that even in the midst of his perfect and copious Augustan syntax, Jones is swept with an unseemly enthusiasm. It was fortunate indeed for Jones's rational bearings that Hebrew had no relation to this linguistic family. He would still argue for the literal truth of Genesis, even giving evidence for the precise location and validity of the myth of the Tower of Babel as an explanation for the scattering of the one true language.

Friedrich Schlegel drew other conclusions: Sanskrit was not only superior to Greek and Latin as a medium for the intellect and the spirit, it "exemplifies the loftiest ideas of the pure world of thought, and displays the entire ground plan of the consciousness, not in figurative symbols, but in direct and immediate clearness and precision."[5] Sanskrit and the mythologies conserved by it were thus a kind of immediate or real archetype of the mind. Learning Sanskrit or any ancient and original language was more than a philological achievement:

> The phenomenon of the soul transporting itself, or, as it were, transported all at once into a language previously quite strange to it, so as to understand any spoken or written composition in it, is certainly not one of ordinary occurrence; and in truth, wherever it manifests itself strongly and decidedly, it closely borders on the marvellous. . . . [It is] a wonderful leap of memory . . . an original recollection.

Such a recollection "is not of a mere foretime, but of eternity, but which in all propriety still admits of being termed a recollection." And this recollection "has brought us to the notion of time and eternity, and to the question of their reciprocal relation."[6] For Schlegel, clearly, Sanskrit provided nothing less than the mental coordinates of a forgotten and whole world.

The consequences of Jones's discovery were developed by the new linguistic science of comparative philology, which discovered a linguistic path from India to the West of Ireland. Seventy years later Darwin's comparative biology would produce a similar effect by claiming that the logic of organic resemblances pointed to a common source. Theories of organic, mythical, and linguistic evolution appeared throughout the nineteenth century. Europeans in particular and people in general were directed by these two Englishmen to look around them and into the past: wherever one looked one could see the ramifications of relatedness. Perhaps for this reason, Europeans also insisted on a rigid distinction between white and colored races, scientific and superstitious cultures, as the older division between Christendom and pagandom began to erode.

Encyclopedic and adventurous thinkers like Hegel and Jung reveled in this wider world but felt a dangerous instability and insecurity. Both philosopher and psychologist saw Indian truths and beauties as a kind of seduction of the senses. Thus the "unearthly beauty" of women immediately following childbirth could be found, Hegel claimed, "in the Indian world; a beauty of enervation in which all that is rough, rigid, and contradictory is dissolved, and we have only the soul in a state of emotion—a soul, however, in which the death of the self-reliant spirit is perceptible."[7] For Hegel, then, India is feminine, beautiful, and fertile, but also effete and decadent. It can only await the dialectic of history to bring Empire and reason in the form of a robust, masculine domination and exploitation: "for it is the necessary fate of Asiatic Empires to be subjected to Europeans."

And in order to fortify his own self-reliant spirit against the enticements of India, Jung brought along an alchemical treatise aboard ship and once having embarked, was careful to avoid "holy men." "I did so because I had to make do with my own truth, not accept from others what I could not attain on my own. . . . Neither in Europe can I make any borrowings from the East, but must shape my life out of myself—out of what my inner being tells me, or what nature brings to me."[8] The threat of India seems to be that it can displace both the self and nature with the force of its persuasive psychologies and mythologies. Both Hegel and Jung come upon it too late to allow it the priority—or at least the antiquity—that it demands.

India, then, is something to be resisted, like sleep, desire, moods whose solutions are always a kind of dissolution. Listening to an Indian *Sadhu*, looking for a *Guru*, invoking the *Upanishads* or the *Bhagavad-Gita* are usually seen as an escape from the strenuous or stoic labors of modernity and as a shunning of the responsibilities borne by those who believe themselves able to distinguish between truth and deception, facts and desires. This is because the idea of "wisdom" is nearly indistinguishable in our thinking from fraud, bogus generalities, mumbo jumbo—a too easy insight into the fundamental nature of things. Like the "eternity" which Europeans await after the fulfillment of history, "wisdom" must be indefinitely deferred.

This thinking of course has familiar undertones: going native, losing one's bearings in an oppressive atmosphere, interpreting delirium as enlightenment, hallucination as truth. These are the dangers awaiting Westerners east of Suez. And yet even, or especially, those Westerners most devoted to the Western project of analysis and description of nature have felt this temptation to turn East, to find what the mine of Sanskrit holds for those who, *in extremis*, find Aristotelian logic neither practical nor possible.

After the first atomic test in the New Mexico desert, J. Robert Oppenheimer repeated to himself Krishna's words from the *Bhagavad-Gita*, "I am become death, the shatterer of worlds."[9] Oppenheimer's words have achieved a certain fabulous quality in the succeeding decades, perhaps because of his collocation of apparent opposites: an ancient mystic scripture and modern science. But his poetic reflections also make a profound appeal to both our senses of a historical and spatial sublime: within the deserts of the new world, a German-born physicist thinks, upon splitting the atom and releasing its energy, of a Sanskrit verse. Reflecting on this classical expression of Hindu mysticism at the very moment the West had realized its divisive and classificatory notion of knowledge by fragmenting matter itself, Oppenheimer indicated that he had (long before he became a critic of the United States's nuclear policy in the early years of the Cold War) already gone native, had despaired of the Western *mission civilisatrice*, had drifted into esoteric vagaries. But by releasing the energy holding matter together, Oppenheimer had, through purely technical means, mastered something described only in Eastern texts: the art of becoming a god.

In Book 10 of the *Bhagavad-Gita*, Arjuna asks Krishna once more to explain his identity with the universe. In the midst of the catalog which follows, Krishna tells Arjuna,

> Of weapons I am the thunderbolt. . . . Of departed ancestors I
> am Aryama, and among dispensers of law I am Yama, the lord
> of death. . . . Of letters I am the letter A [*a-karah*, the first letter],
> and among compound words I am the dual compound. I am
> also inexhaustible time, and of creators I am Brahma. I am all-
> devouring death, and I am the generating principle of all that
> is yet to be.[10]

Krishna's divinity inheres in the atomic composition of matter,
as well as in the architectonics forming the universe: "I am the
supersoul, O Arjuna, seated in the hearts of all living entities.
I am the beginning, the middle, and the end of all beings."

If he saw himself as death, one of Krishna's embodiments,
one of the aspects of universal form, Oppenheimer could do
so only because he had "split" an atom, started a chain reaction
within highly radioactive uranium. He had become death because this first major intrusion into the lattice of matter had
only released destruction.

In both *The Mahabharata*, as staged by Peter Brook,[11] and
the *Srimad Bhagavatam Purana*, as translated by A. C. Bhaktivedanta, one can hear the resonances of this modernist legend. In both works nuclear devices are anachronistically de-
ployed in the place of mysterious, spiritual weapons capable
of an unprecedented destructiveness. In the Brook adaptation,
Karna, the bastard hero of the Kauravas, acquires from Para-
shurama the "formula" for the ultimate weapon inscribed, like
the Vedic scriptures, "on a piece of bark." In the translation
by Bhaktivedanta (the founder of the International Society for
Krishna Consciousness), Krishna, Oppenheimer's apocalyptic
persona, produces the ultimate weapon. When the enemies of
the Pandavas have "thrown the hymns of nuclear energy
[brahmastra]," Krishna tells Arjuna that he must respond in
kind.

> When the rays of the two brahmastras combined, a great circle
> of fire, like the disc of the sun, covered all outer space and the
> whole firmament of the planets. All the populace of the three
> worlds was scorched by the combined force of the weapons.
> Everyone was reminded of the samvartaka fire which takes
> place at the time of annihilation.[12]

The technical apparatuses of nuclear war blend into ancient and mythical narrative: insight into the structure of matter leads to world destruction; to see into the origin is to bring about the end. And so the mythic theme of recurrent worlds, as elaborated by Manu and translated by Jones, is empowered and modernized with nuclear fission and fusion devices.

An atom, as imagined by Democritus and Leucippus and as maintained until the twentieth century, was primarily a word pointing to an idea; literally *a-tom* meant an entity which could not be cut or split. The Indo-European root from which atom derives, *tem*, means cutting, splitting, or slicing, and produces such words as *tome* (a cut portion of a larger volume), *tmesis*, *tonsure*, and, unsurprisingly, *temple*. The Greek prefix "a" negates these senses and maintains that an "atom" is an exception to the general rule that everything can be cut: books, words, hair, and human bodies. Thus Lucretius, whose *De Rerum Natura* takes the atomic theory as its foundation, persistently links the formation of matter out of atoms to the formation of words out of the alphabet. Matter and language observed the same logic of combination: both were simply arrangements from a table of elements. Atomic fission, then, took this philological and physical association into *terra incognita*. By splitting the atom, Lord Rutherford and Oppenheimer had split the idea of atomism, the idea that the world was based on indivisible, that is to say fundamental, elements. The world, both its material and its verbal aspects, was shown to be—even at its most essential—combinatory, relative, connective.

The technical, priestly, and poetic aspects of the Manhattan project and Oppenheimer's reflections on it are implicit within the Indo-European context of the word "atom." Peering into words, like peering into matter, reveals pure association, a system of traces whose origins and definitions are impossible to establish. Seeing this parallel, Joyce—in the middle of *Finnegans Wake*—links his own splitting of the "etym" with Lord Rutherford's splitting of the atom: "The abnihilisation of the etym by the grisning of the grosning of the grinder of the grunder of the first lord of Hurtreford expolodonates through Parsuralia. . . ."[13] What is the relationship, Joyce asks throughout the

*Wake*, between the quantized and qualified subjects of physics and language? What is the relationship or the difference between a material world and a significant world?

By the twentieth century, physics had become a science on its own, not an aspect, as it was for Descartes and Newton, of the wider field of natural philosophy. Physics had become essentially a mathematical explanation of the most fundamental dynamics of bodies and heat. With the discovery and calculation of subatomic particles, the mission of mathematical description and prediction hit a snag. Niels Bohr and Werner Heisenberg discovered and then formalized the fact that the actions and reactions of subatomic particles—those oxymoronic components of an indivisible element—could not be predicted. One had to resort to statistical probabilities of the kind that would be used to describe and predict the actions and reactions of human populations. The uncertainty principle postulated by Heisenberg explained why any attempt to measure both the speed and position of a particle would inevitably alter what it attempted to determine. Physics appeared to have reached the limits of its ability to describe without altering the physical world.

Presented with both the apparently illogical behavior of matter at its most elemental—exactly where one would expect it to be least complex and most mechanical—Bohr and Heisenberg began to consider the philosophic consequences of what they had discovered. Bohr and Heisenberg were especially interested in the ways in which quantum physics showed the limitations of ordinary language and thus the limitations of our ordinary capacity for understanding. Bohr told Heisenberg,

> there can be no descriptive account of the structure of the atom; all such accounts must necessarily be based on classical concepts which, as we saw, no longer apply. You see that anyone trying to develop such a theory is really trying the impossible. For we intend to say something about the structure of the atom but lack a language in which we can make ourselves understood.[14]

Both understood that this was not simply a problem with German or English or Danish: it concerned the basic intellectual significance of their work. When Heisenberg asked Bohr how they could ever hope to understand atoms if they had no language for them, Bohr responded: "I think we may yet be able to do so. But in the process we may have to learn what the word 'understanding' really means." In other words, the long and often interrupted history of atomism, which began with speculation and came into its own through hard calculation and experimentation, will have the effect of transforming us— the way Los Alamos would transform Oppenheimer. Technical sophistication may, for a time, make basic questions like this seem unimportant, but they always have a way of returning.

Bohr, Einstein, and Heisenberg all realized that physics' secession from philosophy in the seventeenth century could not last. Since the limits of purely descriptive and predictive science had been reached, these modern physicists were forced back into philosophic reflection. Einstein maintained that quantum physics was an incomplete theory and thus attempted to re-establish the project of classical physics by joining the theory of relativity with it to form a Grand Unified Theory. Heisenberg developed a subtly skeptical philosophy of representation which maintained the project of quantum physics but admitted its provisional nature. And Bohr began to supplement the Aristotelian logic of noncontradiction with the Taoist-influenced concept of "complementarity," the idea that a single physical phenomenon can be represented accurately in utterly opposing ways that form a tacit unity. The fact that light could be understood both as a wave and a particle was not a contradiction which indicated that one or both of these models had to be wrong: it pointed to a deeper principle within nature, the interpenetration and reciprocity of opposites.

But it was Erwin Schrödinger who saw in the paradoxical findings of quantum physics a parallel with the teachings of the *Upanishads* and the *Bhagavad-Gita*. Before doing the work that earned him the Nobel Prize in 1933, Schrödinger had written a short philosophical treatise entitled *Seek for the Road* (1925) which contests the Western demand that all metaphysical thinking be dismissed. Such a mission is itself a transcendental gesture, since it presumes that scientific knowledge is not itself produced and represented in generalizing, which is to say metaphysical, ways. "All that is apt to happen is that we replace the grand old metaphysical errors with infinitely more *naive* and petty ones."[15] In the same vein Whitehead demonstrated that scientific thought was dominated by what he called the "fallacy of misplaced concreteness,"[16] the naive faith in a correspondence between intellectual forms and "brute matter." Schrödinger believed "that to grasp the basis of phenomena through logical thought may in all probability be impossible, since logical thought is itself a part of phenomena, and wholly involved in them. . . . Logical thinking brings us up to a certain point and then leaves us in the lurch."[17]

And this is precisely what he and other physicists realized in subsequent years: the nature of a physical phenomenon depended on what instruments or what logic one applied to it. Schrödinger explained in his Nobel Address (1933) that quantum physics left one with this conclusion:

> Either this or that (Particle mechanics)
> and
> This as well as that (Wave Mechanics).[18]

Such a conclusion, in logical terms, was nonsense: the entire weight of Western rationality was opposed to it.

For Schrödinger this dilemma confirmed his own deep skepticism about logic's ability to represent the deep structure of the world. He assumed that above all else, the world of mind and objects, words and referents, was essentially and necessarily a single manifestation of Brahman. Logical contradictions do not reveal the limits of the possible; they reveal the limited uses of logic.

Suppose, Schrödinger writes, that you are sitting on a bench in the mountains, regarding the landscape "in the last rays of the departing sun." You might well think, in this moment, of how the mountains existed before you came into the world and will continue to exist after you have ceased to exist. A hundred years before, perhaps someone else sat at this spot, gazing with the same "awe and yearning" at the twilight scene. But, Schrödinger asks,

*Was* he someone else? Was it not you yourself? What is this Self of yours? What necessary condition for making the thing conceived this time into *you* and not someone else, just *you* and not someone else? . . . What justifies you in obstinately discovering this difference—the difference between you and someone else—when objectively what is there is *the same*?

Clearly we cannot maintain this infinite questioning, except by appealing to the modern belief that the ego is an artifact of the body and the cultural forces that surround it. In moments such as this, when one questions persistently and naively the basis of one's self and the *idea* of the self, we come to see, "in a flash, the profound rightness of the basic conviction in Vedanta . . . this life of yours which you are living is not merely a piece of the entire existence, but is in a certain sense the *whole*."

To realize suddenly that one does not own one's life, that one has no title to it, has been described as both an ecstatic and a frightening experience. In such moments of "de-realization" one realizes that every experience is compounded by memory, that our individuality shimmers on the backdrop of mortality like an optical illusion, a *moiré* effect; this is our *Moira*, or fate. It is through such experiences of the unconscious, such instances of an accidental psychic archaeology, that the individual sees through the fictions of particulate existence into the prehistory of our own feelings: "The Self is not so much *linked* with what happened to its ancestors, it is not so much the product, and merely the product, of all that, but rather, in the strictest sense of the word, the SAME THING as all that: the strict, direct continuation of it, just as the Self aged fifty is the continuation of the Self aged forty."[19] And Schrödinger insists that this view is not just metaphorically, but *literally* true: the particulate self is, in actuality, also a wave.

Three years before Oppenheimer's epiphany at Los Alamos, the linguist Benjamin Lee Whorf explored the relations between physical and verbal reality in a remarkable and prophetic essay published by the Theosophical Society of Madras. Supposing that language and matter were aspects of an identical "CAUSAL WORLD," Whorf wrote,

> Just as language consists of discrete lexation-segmentation
> (*Nama-Rupa*) and ordered patternment, of which the latter has
> the more background character, less obvious but more infran-
> gible and universal, so the physical world may be an aggregate
> of quasidiscrete entities (atoms, crystals, living organisms,
> planets, stars, etc.) not fully understandable as such, but rather
> emergent from a field of causes that is itself a manifold of pattern
> and order.

The periodic table and the alphabet are but artificial paradigms
of this field. In process they are the available ground out of
which words and meaning, atoms and matter arise—as in the
gestalt shift prompted in our brains by a two-dimensional representation of a (three-dimensional) cube:

> As physics explores into the intra-atomic phenomena, the dis-
> crete physical forms and forces are more and more dissolved
> into relations of pure patternment. The PLACE of an apparent
> entity, an electron for example, becomes indefinite, interrupted:
> the entity appears and disappears from one structural position
> to another structural position, like a phoneme or any other pat-
> terned linguistic entity, and may be said to be NOWHERE in
> between positions.[20]

The meeting of East and West, the quantum leap, the pho-
nemic leap, the gestalt shift from figure to ground, Schrödinger's "flash" of insight: these are all aspects of what Whorf
calls a CAUSAL WORLD in which material, conscious, and
semantic distinctions arise from the same field. Various Buddhist schools propounded atomic theories of relations and com-
binations, but finally concluded, unlike Western science until
the twentieth century, that atoms were themselves not fundamental, which is to say that they were illusory. According
to the first-century Buddhist teacher Asvaghosa, the material
world can be reduced to atoms, but atoms "will also be subject
to further division" and "all forms of material existence,
whether gross or fine, are nothing but the shadow of parti-
cularization."[21]

Since the thirties, when Bohr and Schrödinger explored the
ways in which quantum physics seemed to challenge the fundamental principles of Western logic and then evoked Taoist

and Vedantic parallels, the parallel has become an increasingly popular theme. Even in a franchise bookstore one will find, despite the limited inventory, titles such as *The Tao of Physics, The Dancing Wu Li Masters: An Overview of the New Physics,* and the like. Physicists and science writers tend to regard such books scornfully, although they recognize that the founders of quantum physics are largely responsible for the comparison of a highly technical physics and an arcane and foreign wisdom literature. Rather than merely disparaging "mysticism"—which of course is at the center of all religions—Jeremy Bernstein sees the arguments offered by Fritjof Capra and others as self-defeating: "To hitch a religious philosophy to contemporary science is the surest route to obsolescence."[22] Bernstein is right to point out that the parallel is a fundamental category error. The behavior of quanta can hardly demonstrate anything fundamental about the world of large-scale objects like cannon balls and human brains. The peculiarity of subatomic particles is precisely that they behave differently than the larger bodies described by Newtonian Laws. So quantum physics cannot say much of relevance about vast concepts like Brahman and Atman, or the Self and the Universe.

The real theme of such books and thinking is mythological in nature and compass: it concerns a reconciliation of the communal validity of science and the private significance of wisdom, and is as well a historical romance wherein the West and the East are reunited in a single, and global, insight into reality. The illustration in Capra's book which juxtaposes Sanskrit scriptures and equations from quantum physics implies this harmonization of calculation and wonder, technique and wisdom. The conceit offered by Bohr and Schrödinger reverses an imperial scenario wherein startled European adventurers discover in the heart of Asia not the outlandish and alien, but their own culture, as Jones did.

Thus after Giza and Persia, Alexander moved toward India with a passion for conquest tempered by fascination. Like his follower Napoleon, he seemed unsure if he wanted to teach or to learn. According to later Greek sources, he had been asked by Aristotle to determine the state of knowledge East of the

Indus—perhaps wondering how many of his teacher Plato's ideas were original.[23] Arrian recounts that long before crossing the Indus, Alexander had affected Oriental clothes, frightening his officers. And when he reached India he spoke with the yogis to learn something of their philosophy and their meditative practices. Arrian concludes dryly that Alexander expressed interest in and respect for them, but that they affected him not in the slightest.[24]

Before and after Alexander, the Western journey East is a theme of both speculation and report. Did Plato, and before him Pythagoras, go to India? And did Jesus' "lost years" include a journey to India, there to inspire the legend of a Western yogi, one Issa? These and other intellectual quests—those of Spinoza, Schopenhauer, Nietzsche—are aspects of a larger theme: the way the exotic and the novel may reveal one's origins. If Egypt has acted consistently as a colossal *memento mori,* a mnemonic of death, distance, and the unthinkable past, India has since Pythagoras appeared as a country of elusive and ineffable, perhaps fraudulent, wisdom.

In many of these instances the search—whether in Egypt or India—concerns a lost or superceded origin, a land of forgotten signs, an order of power and significance abandoned unwittingly for the conveniences of a banal modernity. A collective and personal memory urges one to turn back, and so East, to discover a deeper relationship, usually associated with abject conditions, unsightly rituals, and disturbing parallels. In the eighteenth and nineteenth centuries Europeans went in search of antiquities in the East at the same time that their empires continued to expand. The Lost Tribes, lost wisdom, the lost years of Jesus, the lost original language might all be found there, and the key to the East was India. Even those connected neither with empire nor scholarship felt the call.

The Order of Freemasons in Great Britain, derived from actual masonic guilds concerned with the crafts of surveying, measurement, and design, yielded in the eighteenth century to a speculative Freemasonry dedicated to certain principles of the Enlightenment: the brotherhood of man, a deistic and non-sectarian divinity, and the moral and masonic principles of uprightness and squareness. But the Masons also claimed an ancient heritage, a heritage linking the medieval guilds responsible for the Gothic cathedrals to the builders of the Pyramids, the Hanging Gardens of Babylon, and the Stupas of India. Thus beneath the evidently different mythologies and cultural forms ranging from the subcontinent to Egypt, one single Craft can be traced. The technical values of the Enlightenment and the nineteenth century were thus infused with arcane significance implied by the plumb line, the square, the level, and the compass. This speculative aspect of Masonry thrived as the lodges lost touch with any actual craft or profession. In its place, middle class and aristocratic members alike were inducted into the Knights Templar, the Veiled Prophets of the Enchanted Realm, the Grand Orient of France, the Cryptic Rite, the Ancient Arabic Order of the Mystic Shrine, the Order of the Eastern Star, and many others worldwide. The Masons were dedicated to maintaining the traditions linking East and West, scientific and esoteric knowledge. According to the Masonic historian R. F. Gould, "their prospect of revelations, deeper and deeper at every stage, fostered a hope to reach a supreme goal—the absolute wisdom whose secret was supposed to have been brought from the East."[25]

An especially suggestive digest of this thinking can be found in Freemasons' Hall, a short walk along Coptic Street south and then east of the British Museum. The tomblike building reveals very little to the uninitiated: the walls are high and severe, its doors tall, bronze, and without knobs or handles, its steps leading nowhere unless one is admitted. And above the doors, graven in stone, are the words: "AUDI. VIDI. TACE." Listen, look, and be silent: the teachings of the Craft are evident in the architecture of the Freemasons' Hall in front of you. It thus becomes an archetype of all mystic societies, just as it evokes Noah's Ark, Solomon's Temple, and every other enclosure which represents the whole world created by what the Masons call the First Builder, the great Architect of the Universe.

In Kipling's "The Man Who Would Be King," two former soldiers, seeing the triumph of modern bureaucracy in British

India, set out to conquer a country untouched by colonization, a land Kipling calls Kafiristan. Both wayward Lodge members of the Masonic Order, Daniel Dravot and Peachy Carnehan discover in Kafiristan a lost remnant of their Brotherhood. When Dravot tries the Fellow Craft Grip on a native it is answered. After he has donned his Masonic apron, a priest overturns an idol and discovers "the Master's Mark, same as was on Dravot's apron, cut into the stone."[26] They soon conclude that the alert natives are "sons of Alexander" or perhaps the "Lost Tribes, or something like it, and they've grown to be English." With these credentials, Dravot becomes King and Carnehan his Commander-in-Chief. Leaving India because it has become too constricted by British bureaucracy, the two adventurers find, in the wastes of an Eurasian plain too obscure even to have inspired Western mythologies, Britain, Ancient Greece, and Israel—all awaiting recognition and reunion.

In James Hilton's novel, *Lost Horizon*, and in Frank Capra's film adaptation, a similar meeting of the exotic and the familiar occurs. Hugh Conway, a Foreign Office idealist in 1930s China, is kidnapped and taken to a remote valley in the Himalayas where a utopian community thrives in a perpetual spring. Apparently organized by a Grand Lama whose great age tests the credulity of Conway and his companions, Shangri-La is an ideal, "Eastern" solution to the problems of life. Removed from the stresses and violence of a world moving toward war, the inhabitants of Shangri-La enjoy the natural splendors of their valley and a remarkable health and longevity. Conway is fascinated and seduced by Shangri-La, only to discover that the Grand Lama, this paragon of Oriental inscrutability, is a Belgian Jesuit who wandered into the valley some two centuries earlier and organized a community based on the principles of the Enlightenment. The purpose of Conway's kidnapping is revealed when the Grand Lama, played by a young Sam Jaffee in Capra's film, dies and leaves Shangri-La in his charge.

In the nineteenth and early twentieth century it was still possible to believe that the vast and incompletely charted surface of the earth might conceal such lost or broken connections as those described by Kipling and Hilton. The mystique of maps, evoked by the shapes of shorelines, colors, legends, and names, implied that the world would somehow requite such desires. By Oppenheimer's time, those connections had become obscure indeed, located in the Indo-European etymologies of basic Western words like "reason"; in the wave frequencies of atoms and the Sanskrit scriptures; or at the culmination of history, when East and West would, as Kipling foresaw, meet at "God's great Judgement seat."[27]

# 4

# The Word of Galaxy

And higher, the stars. The new stars of the land of grief.
Slowly the Lament names them: Look, there:
the *Rider*, the *Staff*, and the larger constellation
called *Garland of Fruit*. Then, farther up toward the pole:
*Cradle; Path; The Burning Book; Puppet; Window.*
But there, in the southern sky, pure as the lines
on the palm of a blessed hand, the clear sparking *M.*
that stands for Mothers. . . .

—Rilke, Duino Elegies

On July nights even those unused to looking upward will discover, if only for a moment, a fact that people for thousands
of years could scarcely forget: the sky is filled with stars and
the earth is a cool and dark observatory. Urbanites used to the
general glare of electric light and images within and without
their homes will have to fall back on nearly-forgotten childhood lore and look for constellations. This means to look for
patterns in the spread of stars, patterns which bear the names
of Greek myths or primitive resemblances like those Rilke
names. And there is the thickest of concentrations, too dense
to bear a resemblance to any but a pool of light, or milk, or
even sperm: the Milky Way, our galaxy.

It is a figure of speech to be found in myths around the
world, but the word *galaxy*, its etymologies and articulations,
describe a certain line of intellectual and spiritual descent. The
*via lactea*, as Ovid has it, or the *orbis lactea*, as Cicero does,
led to the medieval "galaxy" only by recalling that the Latin
*lactea* had flowed from the Greek *gála* (milk) and that both
were nourished by a resemblance between human fluids and

celestial brilliance. For before both Greek and Latin words was the early mythological insight that this dense path of stars was like spilt milk: it was, so the Greeks imagined, the milk of Rhea (as in the Greek, *rheo*, to flow) jetted into the sky while she suckled her son Zeus.

In Tintoretto's "The Origin of the Milky Way," this nursery tale is told differently. Here it is not Rhea's, but Hera's breasts which jet milk into the sky. Zeus brings his son Heracles, by Alcmene, to Hera's breasts so that he might become immortal. Tintoretto imagines the scene in an ambiguous way, for Hera seems overtaken, like one of Zeus's many conquests, but she also seems to accept her husband's bastard. As Zeus holds the infant, jets of milk from one unsuckled breast shoot upward to form ten stars, and from the other downward to inseminate the terrene lily. Thus Hera's milk, like Zeus's semen, has a generative and disseminating force upon creation. Where Zeus's emissions inscribe his own narratives within the natural history of the world, Hera's produce the paragons of aspiration and purity: the Milky Way and the lily establish and orient human attempts to transcend the merely sensual and erotic. Heracles will, despite Zeus's attentions, die a painful death for his own infidelities, but the overflow, the excess from this bizarre attempt to steal immortality, establishes the celestial and earthly emblems of longing.

The wondering urbanite is likely to know little of this: he will know that he is looking at a galaxy, one of a countless number. For this is a persistent feature of scientific mythologies: wonder calls for computation and computation induces wonder.

When toward the end of *Ulysses* Leopold Bloom and Stephen Dedalus consider "The heaventree of stars hung with humid nightblue fruit," it is Bloom who is given to calculation. The scientific catechism recounts his

Meditations of evolution increasingly vaster: of the moon invisible in incipient lunation, approaching perigee: of the infinite lattiginous scintillating uncondensed milky way, discernible by daylight by an observer placed at the lower end of a cylindrical shaft 5000 ft deep sunk from the surface towards the centre of the earth: of Sirius (alpha in Canis Maior) 10 lightyears (57,000,000,000,000 miles) distant and in volume 900 times the dimension of our planet: of Arcturus: of the precession of equinoxes: of Orion with belt and sextuple sun theta and nebula in which 100 of our solar systems could be contained.

And as his meditations are driven ever outward in order to comprehend the immensity of what we now call "outer" space, he is, as if by a law of physics, led to

meditations of involution increasingly less vast. . . . Of the eons of geological periods recorded in the stratifications of the earth: of the myriad minute entomological organic existences concealed in cavities of the earth, beneath removable stones, in hives and mounds, of microbes, germs, bacteria, bacilli, spermatazoa: of the incalculable trillions of billions of millions of imperceptible molecules contained by cohesion of molecular affinity in a single pinhead: of the universe of human serum constellated with red and white bodies, themselves universes of void space constellated with other bodies, each, in continuity, its universe of divisible component bodies of which each was again divisible in divisions of redivisible component bodies, dividends and divisors ever diminishing without actual division till, if the progress were carried far enough, nought nowhere was never reached.[1]

The astronomically immense and the infinitesimal have this odd complicity: the zeros multiply to a point well beyond the capacity of people, who generally have difficulty recalling more than seven digits, to visualize or conceptualize them. Thus Pascal, the first person to be frightened by the immensity of the heavens and one of the first to design a modern computer, was led to link *l'infiniment petit et l'infiniment grand*. And it is through these dizzying calculations that Bloom, like anyone else, considers with astonishment how "the years, three score and ten, of allotted human life formed a parenthesis of infinitesimal brevity." What place has a human life in this beehive of zeros?

If modern scientists, like Bloom or the enthusiasts who dramatize their reflections on television, are driven to calculate the incalculable or enumerate the innumerable, this is because Westerners have been particularly prone to confuse the eternal with the infinite. In an antimetaphysical age it would be inevitable that eternity, the idea of an existence without respect to the fiction of Time, should be linked to an endless progression of zeros, to Infinity. Incanted like a mantra, words like "billions of billions" nevertheless serve as a perfectly secular invitation to consider sacred themes like the Creation, the Apocalypse, and Eternity. And yet this enumeration is nothing more than the marking of decimals by the consummate figure of nullity, the zero. It should not be surprising that the zero, usually attributed to Arab mathematicians, originated in India with the philosophy of endlessly renewing universes and the yogic and meditative approaches to reality and eternity as emptiness (Śūnyatā).

For no one has ever *looked at the stars*, if one means by that an objective or an impassioned inspection. "To look at" is a figure of speech which presupposes a discarded theory of optics which holds that our eyes emit rays of light toward perceived objects. To see the stars, to be looked at *by the stars*, is to be penetrated and illuminated by starlight. If the neurons in our brains, as Sir Charles Sherrington has suggested,[2] could be compared to the Milky Way, perhaps that is because for every star in the galaxy there is approximately one neuron in our brains: approximately $10^{11}$, or one trillion.[3] This is of course less a significant correlation, or even a "coincidence," than a traditional observation of the correspondence of the microcosmos and macrocosmos. The correspondence itself is less significant than the fact that scientists, who affect an immunity to the lure of secret symmetries and parallels, should have made it.

The relationship between the galaxy of stars and some inner principle of the Self (the soul, destiny, conscience, the brain) would appear to be the metaphoric axis of any attempt to understand man's place in the universe. "The fault, dear Brutus, is not in our stars, / But in ourselves, that we are underlings." Cassius's remarks, even while denying the tenets of astrological destiny, situate the very notion of a truthful understanding of men and women as metaphysical beings within a certain astral contract. For how is one to grasp this obvious but neglected relationship between an infinitely alien world represented by the scatter of stars on a summer night and the intimate and yet somehow elusive "self"?

Whether one searches through scientific, philosophic, or mythological sources, one will always find elemental and metaphysical assertions about the nature and position of people in relation to the stars. Modern scientific theory holds, without the slightest romantic embellishment, that our bodies are the remnants of the originative astral explosion called the Big Bang. We are, to be etymologically precise, a disaster (*dis*+*astro*), a falling out with, or fall-out from, the stars. But long before science determined that this originative disaster was the origin of the universe, the Gnostics had postulated that human beings "fell" into their bodies the way light falls from the stars into the earth. Hans Jonas explains this image of falling: "the soul or spirit, a part of the first Life or Light, fell into the world or into the body."[4] El Chatibi of the Harranites, as cited by Jonas, writes that "the Soul turned toward matter, she became enamored of it, and burning with the desire to experience the pleasures of the body, she no longer wanted to disengage herself from it. Thus the world was born. From that moment the Soul forgot herself. She forgot her original habitation, her true center, her eternal being." In both scientific and Gnostic accounts there is indeed something essential in the casual glance that becomes a prolonged and wondering gaze toward the stars: we are looking toward a greater expanse of self, toward our mother, milk, matter. In this way, after leaving the starry mausoleum in Ravenna, Jung unconsciously dramatized his link with a greater self, his anima, Galla, whose name must have inspired the association.

In the 1970s Erich von Daniken's extremely popular books provided a new, technologized Gnosticism by arguing that the gods and goddesses of ancient myths were in fact ancient astronauts. Following in the tradition of anthropologists such as Frobenius, von Daniken argued that the gods were not simply imaginative projections of psychological concerns, but the founders of mundane civilizations. Developing the premise that myths have an actual basis in history, he revived the Gnostic theme of a celestial descent and a corporeal imprisonment. He saw in prehistoric figures the adumbrations of our own technological modernity; thus technology plays its role in the recovery of memory. According to this theory the geometric styles of hieratic art are, in fact, schematic and informative, and mandalas and cosmic disks are to be seen as flying saucers.

In the last years of his life, Jung had pondered the world-wide outbreak of UFO sightings and concluded that they were an expression in archetypal terms of an alien redeemer. Modern observers, looking into the sky on a summer's night, discovered their own deepest fears and hopes displayed in the Gnostic idiom, now inflected by human technologies projected onto other worlds and eras. Jung believed the sightings to be a collective hallucination of a salvation that would require the severest kind of faith and adherence: those bringing word of their sightings or abductions would have to be as courageous as the early Christians.[5]

But von Daniken, discarding the psychological hypothesis, simply argues in direct and naive fashion that the various mysterious phenomena—from the Pyramids to a "landing pad" in the Andes, from petroglyphs of "astronauts" to a Byzantine map whose accuracy could only be achieved by a satellite—are all instances of an unimagined genesis. The Gnostic aspects of his myth appeal to the sublime prospect of history finally upended and reversed: the twentieth century's technological conceits are but the faint echoes of an unthinkable posterity which returns us to the stars. If the statues on Easter Island were erected by marooned aliens, longing, in von Daniken's original German, for a *Zurück zu den Sternen*, then our own banal modernity must also be fabulous and deserving of wonder.

Lucifer, who carried the light (*lux* + *ferre*, to bear) to earth, and Prometheus who stole it; the fallout from the Big Bang and the Gnostic "fall, sinking, and capture" of Spirit; all are narratives implicit within the physics of light. They all explain how it is that we should look, with something ranging from curiosity or rapture, toward the galaxy. It would be idle then to maintain which metaphysical or mythological account is primary or most influential. For long before the recorded documents of Gnosticism, Platonism, and *Genesis* there is an elemental story to be deciphered in the fall of starlight. It is there one will read the pretext for gods, invisible or plentiful, hidden in the depths of space; of influences, beneficial or malevolent, concealed in stars; of desires, enraptured or frightened, provoked by the paradox of distance and immediacy.

The figure of a person rapt in contemplation of the stars reveals a refinement of the conventions of intimacy, which are too often associated with acts of introspection. To confront the ocean or a desert—any inquiry into the vast—seems to have, paradoxically, an aura of the private. In the Argentine film *Man Facing Southeast*, directed by Eliseo Subiela, an inmate in an asylum whose presence cannot be accounted for in the roster of patients perplexes the weary psychiatrist by his prolonged vigils in the courtyard. Unmoving as a sphinx gazing into space and time, this ascetic and intent man regards the southeastern skies, his head at a fixed and unwavering angle, in apparent anticipation and communion. When he explains to the psychiatrist that he is an alien fallen from the sky, it seems as if the psychological metaphor of "alienation" is simply being enlivened in a literal way. But the alien's effect on his fellow inmates changes the psychiatrist's mind: they follow the alien about, discern his powerful but merciful presence, and are soon coming to him, not the physician, to confess their sins and be healed. Soon the doctor becomes convinced that the alien is indeed a kind of fallen god, a "cybernetic Christ" whose grace is conveyed in the medium of a hologram.

It is this traditional Gnostic theme of fall and the longing for return which makes his alienness so familiar to the madmen who gather around him. Their own alienation allows them, rather more quickly than the disenchanted psychiatrist, to recognize that Orontes's condition is their own. Thus as the alien continues to gaze at the stars, he becomes more human, until his origins, real as they appear to be, begin to merge with the persistent yet unreal sense of a lost home, a certain disquiet familiar to those who are only mad.

In *Genesis* Yahweh resorts to this prospect of the stars when he seeks to enter into a contract with Abram and his children.

But before turning to the stars, Yahweh will point his creature toward the earth, saying to him, "And I will make thy seed as the dust of the earth: so that if a man can number the dust of the earth, *then* shall thy seed also be numbered" (14.16). The seed of Abram will become as innumerable, as *incalculable*, as the dust of the earth that the Creator used in the creation of Adam. Then, after Abram builds an altar to him, Yahweh brings him "forth abroad, and said, Look now toward heaven, and tell the stars, if thou be able to number them: and he said unto him, So shall thy seed be" (15.5). The Covenant that God makes with the renamed Abraham, the contract that forms the axis of the true discourse connecting earth with heaven and heaven with earth, can only be struck with the incalculable in the balance. The One True God can be brokered by the infinite, but not by the eternal. Yahweh does not offer immortality for the souls in a heavenly city. He promises that Abraham's seed, these metaphors of Abraham, will multiply *like* the dust of the earth and the stars of the heaven. It is a worldly Covenant because Yahweh is Himself unaffected by it; his spirit, his body remain alien and unreachable.

In Plato's *Timaeus* the metaphor is granted the dignity and promise of a myth. The Demiurge who fashioned the universe fashions the immortal part of the soul:

> he turned once more to the same mixing bowl wherein he had mixed and blended the soul of the universe, and poured into it what was left of the former ingredients, blending them this time in somewhat the same way, only no longer so pure as before, but second or third in degree of purity. And when he had compounded the whole, he divided it into souls equal in number with the stars, and distributed them, each to its several star.[6]

There the soul rides in a chariot and is shown "the nature of the universe" and taught "the laws of Destiny." From this exposure to the universe and by virtue of his substantial identity with it, the individual soul once incarnated will come to knowledge by an essential recollection (*Anamnesis*) of reality. It follows that his Destiny will be determined by his ability to maintain and act according to his inmost recollection of the universe. Once shown the nature of reality and taught the laws which will determine his future lives, the soul is "sown into the instruments of time"—"some in the Earth, some in the Moon"—there to begin the earthly rounds of experience. According to the Platonic account then, however mythological and illustrative, people who look to the stars are lost in a sublime recollection of their origins and their destiny. "This is how," Giorgio de Santillana explains, "the archaic idea of 'going to heaven' re-enters Western thought, for it did not belong either to Hebrew or to Homeric tradition."[7] And why is it that it "re-enters"? Because the "archaic idea" is indissociable from the fall of starlight and the returning gaze of mythological peoples: our metaphysics of eternity has this substantial and recurrent foundation. Thus when Dedalus and Bloom look at the "heaventree of stars hung with humid night-blue fruit," Joyce introduces a certain skepticism about the intrinsic nature of their identities by placing them under the stars: the two Irishmen, one with a Greek name and one a converted Jew, are like the reincarnations of Daedalus and Ulysses.

This identity, whether metaphysical or metaphorical, between the principles of greatest inwardness and greatest outwardness told in these astral narratives are instances of an even more fundamental pattern. Whether in myth or in science, the appreciation and the attainment of truth concerns the meeting between two such principles, either long separated or only distantly linked by a sequence of relations. This would be an example of the correspondence theory of truth: the assumption that truth is the confirmation of an occurrence when languages, images, numbers, or heroes are reconciled with one another across the meeting place of an equal sign, a colon, or a terrestrial or celestial topos.

When Einstein produced the formula $E = mc^2$ to express the fundamental truth of General Relativity, a whole panoply of mythic and scientific elements were assembled, opposed, and reconciled at the same moment. Although Einstein's purpose was to establish the terms of the relationship between energy and mass, between the dynamic and the substantial aspect of the universe, what could be called the meta-function of this equation was no less significant. This reflexive aspect of the equation demonstrated that physical protagonists like Energy, Mass, and Light could be reconciled with the working of the world and with human symbols such as the Roman letters E, M, and C, the number system devised by ancient Hindu mathematicians, and human conceptions of velocity and squaring. For in a larger sense, larger even than the circumscribed relevance which he himself maintained for General Relativity, Einstein's achievement was to have brought the Universe and the Mind, matter and abstraction, into a relationship between signs, according to the velocity of the most powerful emblem of truth ever invoked.

Those inclined to see an inevitable effect of destiny in human representations would scarcely be able to ignore the fact that the "light" invoked by Einstein and the "Fiat Lux" of Yahweh are drawn from the same dictionary of elements. And the space of correspondence, the equivalence of opposing forces, upon which the truth depends, is little more than a transparency: an equal sign, a colon, a copula are like a pause, a mere breath between worlds.

The space between worlds, variables, and constants, the gap upon which all truth depends, is like a fulcrum which allows two opposing weights and forces to cooperate, with the aid of nothing more than the touch of a finger, in overcoming gravity. The truths of correspondence are a little like this: ponderous weights (Energy, Mass; I think, I am) are lifted and lowered only because they find their center in absence. As Lao Tzu reminds us, the cartwright's art is most focused not on the rim, the spokes, the hub, or the axle, but on the space he must leave between the hub and the axle: it is there that the wheel turns and the cart moves.[8]

What this means is that the essential, the irreducible, or the fundamental point in the world, in discourse, and in machines is very like something which is not there: an opening, a space, a gap which *joins*. If the wheel and axle were to fall into the background, one could see this space where the movement is as a ring of light. The doubled bars signifying equivalence, the penstroke of a comma signifying apposition, the conjugations

of "to be," all are like this empty space suddenly become il-
luminating when they are informed by an act of mind signifying relationship. The space between the eye and a star, or
between the soul and its origin, is symbolically no different
from such arbitrary signs of distance and immediacy, difference
and identity. For this reason, the most resonant and enduring
of metaphysical values (the soul, freedom, immortality) are
always appreciated in dramas of separation, loss, and longing.
Since these principles cannot be plotted according to any single
and exclusive point within Euclidean and Newtonian Space,
their reality has become more and more psychologized. They
are now to be found only in the appendices of history where
spirits, souls, chimeras, destinies, antiquated cosmologies, esoteric knowledges, and dead languages are conserved and an-
notated. But to gaze at the galaxy (or the sea, or a landscape,
or the pupils of two eyes) is a way of re-acquainting ourselves
with their conditioned existences, with the uncanny fact that
absence, distance, and emptiness represent our deepest desires.
This is what longing means.

Judaism, Platonism, and Gnosticism have refracted this starlight according to their different purposes and cultural prece-
dents. In each account, however, one can see that the stars and
the individual self are bound by a kind of contractual logic. By
the time that Kant wrote his *Critique of Practical Reason* (1788),
this relationship had become purely analogical, but no less
significant, and perhaps no less metaphysical for that. I am
referring, of course, to the famous passage at the end of the
second of his *Critiques* where Kant inscribed perhaps his most
memorable words:

> Two things fill the mind with ever new and increasing admi-
> ration and awe, the oftener and more steadily we reflect on
> them: *the starry heavens above and the moral law within* [*der
> bestirnte Himmel über mir, und das moralische Gesetz in mir*]. I
> have not to search for them and conjecture them as though they
> were veiled in darkness or were in the transcendent region be-
> yond my horizon; I see them before me and connect them di-
> rectly with the consciousness of my existence. The former begins
> from the place I occupy in the external world of sense, and
> enlarges my connection therein to an unbounded extent with

worlds upon worlds and systems of systems, and moreover into limitless times of their periodic motion, its beginning and continuance. The second begins from my invisible self, my personality, and exhibits me in a world which has true infinity, but which is traceable only by the understanding and with which I discern that I am not in a merely contingent but in a universal and necessary connection, as I am also thereby with all those visible worlds.[9]

More than memorably concluding Kant's argument that people possess an intrinsic moral law, this passage symbolizes the central task of his whole philosophy: to establish certain metaphysical possibilities secure from the skepticism of empirical and scientific philosophies. And what is essentially Kantian about this assertion is that it is not asserted dogmatically after metaphysical intuition nor empirically after sensuous perception: it is poised at the still, empty space of an analogy aligning the self and the galaxies—a subject upon which Kant had much to say since he was the first person to postulate their existence.

Kant's "Universal Natural History and Theory of the Heavens, Or an Essay on the Constitution and Mechanical Origin of the Whole Universe Treated According to Newton's Principles" (1755) argued that the so-called "fixed stars" were not randomly scattered like the milky seed of Genesis. They formed instead, Kant argued, "a certain plane which must be conceived as drawn through the whole heavens, and by their being very closely massed in it they present that streak of light which is called the Milky Way (*die Milchstrasse*)."[10] But not only did Kant, in a manner so characteristic of his genius, realize that the Milky "Way" was but a disc of stars seen through its radius, he realized that "the fixed stars are so many suns, centres of similar systems, in which everything may be arranged just as grandly and with as much order as in our system; and that the infinite space swarms with worlds, whose number and excellency have a relation to the immensity of their Creator." That a star could be a sun, that the periphery, however spectacular, could by a single blink of the eyes, in an *Augenblick*, become a center: this was the fundamental Kantian insight. We can look ahead to his *Prolegomena for any Future Metaphysics* and its famous forward with a greater sense of how Kant conceived of his work. It was, he claimed without any sense of pride, a "Copernican revolution" that he had achieved.

This revolution was achieved by a tactic often used by Enlightenment thinkers: by diminishing nature one could aggrandize humanity. The airy platitudes of secular reason were weighted with the certain virtues of demystification: just as Christianity thrived by uprooting or transforming pagan (that is "provincial" or "country") mythologies, so the Enlightenment won authority by shining in (and vaporizing) the "darkness." Thus a commentator on Kant writes,

> The starry heavens seem sublime because man first feels reduced by them to impotency, only to rise above them again when he knows that his rational nature, which comprehends them, is not subdued but heightened by the magnitude and power revealed in them. He erroneously attributes a sublimity to nature which actually belongs only to his rational being; the sublimity ascribed to nature is a clue to his own superiority to nature.[11]

Just as ethics supercedes astrology and rationalism surpasses naturalism, so do human beings, as metaphysical principles, emerge from the welter of matter and the external mysteries of distance, immensity, and the abysses they evoke.

And yet there is a disquieting remainder, a bit of biography which falls, unsurprisingly, to the foot of the commentator's page. After mentioning that Kant had linked the stars and human morality before in several other works, the commentator writes that "the two were deeply connected in Kant's own life of feeling, no doubt having first been joined by Kant's mother." He then adds this apparent "supplement" to his argument in the form of a footnote: "In the famous statement on his reverence for his mother . . . he speaks of her as having 'planted and nourished the seed of the good' and 'opened [his] heart to the impressions of nature.' " Kant's mother can hardly be blamed for confounding her son's arguments, but this is what she does. For if the good can be "planted" and "nourished" like a "seed" and the "heart" can be "impressed" with the force of nature, can it be seriously maintained that the individual conscience is "superior" to the world of nature and the feeling of the mother's breast in the philosopher's mouth? And what if this seed of goodness were, as we read in Genesis, comparable to the stars and both were of the order of a divine contract? For God's promise to Abraham, the original covenant beyond which no search for the originating word of Western ethics can go, is irreducibly metaphoric: it clouds progeny, semen, and the stars in one scattered portrait of the future. For here too is not only the Covenant but the breaking of the Covenant, the Diaspora, and perhaps even the Holocaust—of both the Jewish people and of what Kant would have called "Man." One could also say that this was the origin not only of Ethics (and the Moral Law within) but of astrology. For Kant's mother taught young Kant to open "his heart to the impressions [and thus the influences] of nature." This is a teaching that comes with a mother's milk: *gála, galaxy.*

But it was not one Kant could learn. Time and again, in his ethics and aesthetics, Kant can establish human principles of conscience and the sublime only by insisting that people must remain "superior" to the displays, even the examples, of the heavens:

> Sublimity, therefore, does not reside in any of the things of nature, but only in our own mind, in so far as we may become conscious of our superiority over nature within, and thus also over nature without us (as exerting influence upon us). Everything that provokes this feeling in us, including the *might* of nature which challenges our strength, is then, though improperly, called sublime, and it is only under presupposition of this idea within us, and in relation to it, that we are capable of attaining to the idea of the sublimity of that Being which inspires deep respect in us, not by the mere display of its might in nature, but more by the *faculty which is planted within us* of estimating that might without fear, and of regarding our estate as exalted above it [italics mine].[12]

Is it simply by a deficiency of language, or by an inconsequent use of a metaphor, that Kant separates human beings from nature only to join them again with remarks that conceptualize the origin of a moral faculty as a kind of insemination and growth? Or is it that a "mind" such as Kant conceived, alien to the order of nature, only analogically inclined to the stars, could scarcely conceive of "itself" except through metaphors of fertilization, gestation, birth, and growth. Since "God," the "Being" toward which "Man" is drawn, even as it is repulsed by nature, could be defined strictly as the most powerful resistance to metaphor, representation, and illustration, Kant had no other field to plough. Today he would doubtless have employed metaphors drawn from artificial intelligence or cybernetics. Even so, he would only be enticed into secondary sets of metaphors borrowed from mathematics and navigation.

Freud, usually so respectful of his philosophic fathers, could only mock this sexless philosopher whose movements have been linked in legend with the turning wheels of Königsberg's many clocks:

> The stars are indeed magnificent, but as regards conscience, God has done an uneven and careless piece of work, for a large majority of men have brought along with them only a modest amount of it or scarcely enough to be worth mentioning. We are far from overlooking the portion of psychological truth that is contained in the assertion that conscience is of divine origin; but the thesis needs interpretation.[13]

In these remarks from chapter 31 of the *New Introductory Lectures*, Freud is ready to cite Kant, the rationalist who enshrined an emerging bourgeois ethics within the stars, only as an ironic precursor of his new science of the soul. "The thesis needs interpretation," he writes. Indeed. But by chapter 35 Freud has "forgotten" that he has already humored Kant one hundred pages earlier:

> I may remind you of Kant's famous pronouncement in which he names, in a single breath, the starry heaven and the moral law within us [see p. 525 above]. However strange this juxtaposition may sound—for what have the heavenly bodies to do with the question of whether one human creature loves another or kills him?—it nevertheless touches on a great psychological truth.

He then returns, once again, to an explanation of the internalization of the father's authority into the superego, the only "conscience" of which Freud will admit.

But what is "the great psychological truth" concealed in Kant's pronouncement? Having "overlooked" the earlier reference, as his editor James Strachey has it, to Kant, Freud may have had more on his mind than he could allow his pen to express. Following Freud's own example in looking for the source of a parapraxis, we might return to the page from the *Critique of Practical Judgment* which he recalls so vividly. There Kant explains that before a scientific or rational view of the outer spectacle and the inner rule could be achieved, human beings had to pass through two absurdities:

> The contemplation of the world began from the noblest spectacle that the human senses present to us, and that our understanding can bear to follow in their vast reach; and it ended—in astrology. Morality began with the noblest attribute of human nature, the development and cultivation of which give a prospect of infinite utility; and ended—in fanaticism or superstition.[14]

This is perhaps where Freud trips.

For if there was one purpose Freud had in this late introduction to his science, it was to defend it against contemporary charges of occult, superstitious, or fanatical determinism—hence his injunctions against "lay" or "wild" psychoanalysis. It must have been all the more frustrating to imagine that psychoanalysis had already been charged, dismissed, and superceded a century and a half earlier by the greatest of the German philosophers as an adjunct of . . . astrology.

But this is a word he will not utter in his lectures, although "astronomy" is much in evidence: "No reader of an account of astronomy will feel disappointed and contemptuous of the science if he is shown the frontiers at which our knowledge of the universe melts into haziness" (28). In devising a *Traumdeutung*, Freud had tried to offer more than a "hazy" "interpretation" in the fashion of an astrologist or an oracle: he provided an "explanation" (*eine Deutung*).

Perhaps "the great psychological truth" Freud found in Kant's remarks was immanent in this correlation of the stars and the inner "law" in people. Freud only disputed the origin of this law, seeing in the figure of the stars an emblem of "the same father (or parental agency) which gave the child life and guarded him against its perils, taught him as well what he might do and what he must leave undone." Freud can himself, in other words, reject *and* accept Kant's "parental agency" by being "taught" "what he might do and what he must leave undone." Freud had already raided the preserves of the occult by devising a grammar for the language of dreams, and in these same *New Introductory Lectures* he considered the possibility or the meanings of telepathy. By interpreting Kant's metaphor in this fashion, Freud reveals his "great psychological truth" as a proto-psychoanalysis *inscribed in the stars.*

Astrology presumes that the relationship between the individual subject and the universe is a necessary and determining one. Undeterred by the sublime, if immense, nature of the requisite analysis, astrology has not renounced, as any modern science would, this fundamental premise that each human subject comes "out" of the world, not "into" it. By plotting the position of the stars and the planets at the time of one's birth, an astrologist is in effect charting an image of the whole infant, the whole speechless world from which it has emerged. Like Platonic and Gnostic accounts, astrology begins by insisting that the whole is always relevant to all of its parts—whether one calls them souls, selves, or persons. Astrology is in other words a psychoanalysis carried out in the medium of what science would later call astronomy. By looking at the stars we look into our own minds, and into the vast unconscious from which they emerge, for a time, in the guise of an ego. Founded on both observation and introspection, astrology formalizes the unconscious principles of mythologies into the science and art of interpretation, *eine Sterndeutung,* like *eine Traumdeutung.*

If the Gnostics believed that our egos have fallen from the stars like light, there to be trapped in animal bodies and delusions of our identity with flesh and matter, the mythologizers of the Milky Way imagined that human goddesses and gods jetted milk and semen into an empty space. Both insisted that the "distance" separating them was not evidence of alienation but the sign of an essential bond.

The effect of destiny initiated by the stars is like the fate or *Moira* which greatly concerned the classical world. Both words suggest a fact or deed awaiting its realization in time. Like the stars, the fate or destiny of an individual is already *written*, but it must be read in time. It is the gap between the departure of light from a star and its arrival in the eye of its earthbound and fated observer. Thus to see a star is to remember it: the distance between the star and its subject are complemented by the antiquity of the light which finally arrives. The soul of Plato's *Timaeus* and the Gnostics are allied with distances, imprisonment, forgetting, and fitful memory, as if the medium of the soul were absence and emptiness, and as if it existed only insofar as it is suspended in the space and the time between worlds. In the same way, the immateriality and mysterious provenance of human conscience, as imagined by Kant, can only be properly appreciated by a kind of psychic or astral archaeology which uncovers or evokes this expanse.

Cosmologists have proposed recently what they call an "anthropic principle" to explain the mysteries of how and why it was that the universe appeared. According to Stephen Hawking, "We see the universe the way it is because we exist."[15] Thus the Big Bang took place fifteen or twenty billion years ago because it takes that long for human beings to evolve bodies and intelligences capable of making such a determination. And the more profound metaphysical questions (*Why* is the universe the way it is? Why does it exist at all?) are simply enough answered: if the universe did not exist exactly as it does, we would not be here to pose such questions. The anthropic principle, whether in its weak (physical) or strong (metaphysical) forms, assumes that final causes are inherent in the invisible bonds linking the galaxy with a casual, studious, or impassioned regard. John Gribbin and Martin Rees write, "So the fact that we exist tells us, in a sense, what conditions are like inside stars and in the Universe at large."[16] Like the tentative tracing of a constellation in a scatter of stars, this scientific hypothesis discovers in apparent randomness a compelling pattern and an elusive necessity: light, life, seed, milk, and the distant origins of conscience.

# 5

# The Metaphor of the Shell

et bientôt le coquillage formel, cette coquille d'huître ou cette tiare bâtarde, ou ce ⟨⟨couteau⟩⟩, m'impressionera comme un enorme monument, en même temps colossal et précieux, quelque chose comme le temple d'Angkor, Saint-Maclou, ou les Pyramides, avec une signification beaucoup plus étrange que ces trop incontestables produits d'hommes.
—Francis Ponge, "Notes sur un Coquillage"

To discover a seashell half-buried in the sands, not of a seashore, but of a desert—this is both a scientific and a prophetic occasion. A desert becomes, through the agency of a single organic sign, an ancient sea. The shimmering mirages of retreating waters collect in a vision of the deluge, which is to say the seas which once covered the earth. The great American desert and the receding seas imagined by Louis Agassiz are poised as on the lip of a shell, the threshold of outside and inside, air and water, present and past. One can see and touch such a labial margin in the shell one is holding, there where the horny and limey exterior turns suddenly inward to become the seductive sheen of its precious interiors. It is as if a stone had become alive in one's hands.

Fables of the seashell originate in this margin between land and sea, the present and the past, because the shell is itself a contradiction where inside and outside seem to revolve on a single axis. And if one places a shell to the ear, is this because one expects that it will speak, sing, chant, breathe, or echo? Is it because a shell resemble the ear, or that one expects the pleasure of listening to the sea? Or does one expect that this resemblance can recall one's own ear and enable us to listen to *it*? As every child knows, the shell has its own song, which is the song of the sea, the rising and the crashing of waves. Only later, at about twelve, does one learn that one has been listening to the blood rushing in one's head. For some the matter ends there in the form of an explanation. The persistent child knows that the story has only begun: he will have suspected that the sea is inside of him, not as in a figure of speech or as in an epiphenomenon, but in another way.

With the exception of bivalves such as clams and oysters (whose form suggests the mouths they feed rather than the ears their gastropod relatives allow us to hear), seashells have consistently figured in human representations as both an ancestral hearing and an authoritarian sounding. In the *Bhagavad-Gita*, before the battle between the Pandavas and Kurus and before the instructions which Krishna gives Arjuna, it is the conch shells which sound the calls to battle and the "transcendental conch shells" (*divyau shankhau*) of Krishna and Arjuna which indicate their coming victory. The conch shell is a primal trumpet in such epic narratives, as it is for the boys stranded on a desert island in Golding's *Lord of the Flies*: in both it is the authority of the sea, its vastness and unruliness, and the mystery of the shell's form, which combine to establish its power. And it is in this same, if inverted way, that the shell, when placed to the ear, would seem to speak of its own marine past.

Since the shell is a symbol of authority, speech, and hearing, which is to say a symbol of prophecy, one can begin to understand its spiraling form as an allegory of all origins and their ends. While such words as "origin" suppose an exemplary "arising" (*origo*) from which all else flows, it is the shell which suggests another model: a spiral, a vortex, a whirlpool from which and out of which things both appear and disappear.

The prophetic and the memorable, the future and the past are in this way conserved within the inward and outward whorls of a shell, as if within the covers of a book. And yet the pages of this book are themselves blank and nacreous, streaked by blues perhaps but without trace or inscription. Its form is thus apocalyptic in the sense that it speaks of destruction and revelation, and suggests how each can be the consequence of the other. More ancient, more marvelous, more unfathomable than the wonders of the ancient world, as Ponge writes, the seashell is, like them, a recollection of life's earliest architectures and enigmas.

When in *The Prelude* Wordsworth takes account of books and their role in the growth of a poet's mind we should not then be surprised to find an elaborate dream-allegory centered on the figures of a stone and a shell. Wordsworth begins by expressing his fear that the world and human culture might survive an apocalyptic destruction but that the expressions of mind might well be lost: "all the adamantine holds of truth, / By reason built, or passion, which itself / Is highest reason in a soul sublime . . . / Where would they be?"[1] He wonders why such human truths must "lodge in shrines so frail" as books, just after referring to the "adamantine holds" built by reason. It is as if his hyperbolic metaphors (stone holds or castle keeps and dungeons) were canceled out by his more prosaic realization that Shakespeare, Homer, and Milton exist as ink on paper or not at all: so much is obvious in an age which has put its trust in external marks. Pages awash in a stream, a book cast in the sea, a parchment curling in flames: these are the likely fates of human meditations consigned to writing. It would appear that the truth of bard and sage is only metaphorically a combination of a stone and a hold—a hollowed stone—or a shell. In reality, Wordsworth fears, metaphor is only an impotent semblance, but he hopes that it is a strict mnemonic device which can guide his faltering account of the growth of his own mind.

Wordsworth then relates how having told a "Friend" of his fears, he is told in his turn a prophetic dream: his Friend had been reading *Don Quixote* in a cave by the sea when the same fears had come to him. Considering the eternal truth of "Poetry and geometric Truth," he falls asleep and dreams he is in an "Arabian waste / A Desart." Then an Arab of the Bedouin tribes appears atop a camel, holding a lance forward, and under each arm two portentous symbols: a stone and a shell:

> the Arab told him that the Stone,
> To give it in the language of the Dream,
> Was Euclid's Elements; "and this," said he,
> "This other," pointing to the Shell, "this Book
> Is something of more worth." And, at the word,
> The Stranger, said my Friend continuing,
> Stretch'd forth the Shell towards me, with command
> That I should hold it to my ear; I did so,
> And heard that instant in an unknown Tongue,
> Which yet I understood, articulate sounds,
> A loud prophetic blast of harmony,
> An Ode, in passion utter'd, which foretold
> Destruction to the Children of the Earth,
> By deluge now at hand.

The Arab then tells his Friend that he will bury the book of elements which describes in the eternal laws of geometry man's relationship to the stars, and the other divine book of poetry which contains joyful and hopeful consolation for people in their enigmatic isolation from the living world of nature. Following the Arab in hopes of guidance, the Friend sees him "riding o'er the Desart Sands, / With the fleet waters of the drowning world / In chace of him, whereat I wak'd in terror, / And saw the Sea before me; and the Book, / In which I had been reading, at my side."

Sea and desert, Wordsworth and Friend, shell and stone, geometry and prophecy, Book and Dream, Arab and Quixote— all these are both set apart and then apocalyptically joined: within the scope of prophecy and dream, quotidian oppositions are easily bridged or annulled. And yet chief among these is one that Wordsworth perhaps concealed for his own private appreciation. In the first drafts the dream is attributed to a "Philosophical Friend" who one would immediately assume to be Coleridge; in the 1805 edition, it is simply a "Friend"; by 1850 the dream had become his own.

But the Philosophical Friend who told Wordsworth his dream was not Coleridge, who had tried to isolate the truth value of poetry from the withering critiques of early modern science. He was, instead, one of the inventors of modern science and philosophy, the man who had, according to Boileau, cut poetry's throat. For, as J. W. Smyser has persuasively argued, this dream derives from Descartes's famous dreams of November 10, 1619, when the philosopher felt he had received a vocation from the "Spirit of Truth" to undertake a revision of all knowledge, using the elements of geometry and mathematics as a foundation.[2] If there is an irony in this dream, it is a sinuous and perplexing one, rather like the turnings in the shell of the nautilus, the very type of the mysteries of the sea, poetry, and geometry.

On that night in November, 1619, Descartes, recently a soldier and a philosopher by avocation, dreamed three dreams, sketchily recorded and reconstructed by his biographer Baillet. On the basis of these dreams, Descartes was able to establish the foundations of what we know as modern science. But the idea that truth could come from dream and that Cartesian certainty could derive from universal doubt are but the last turns in this spiraling irony. In fact, the sequence of dreams has the archetypal form of religious conversion. In the first dream, Descartes finds himself in a courtyard driven by an "impetuous wind, which, carrying him away in a kind of vortex, made him spin three or four times on the left foot."[3] Spinning like a top, the man who would later propose the theory of the vortex then seeks shelter in a college church but is distracted by various passersby, and awakens, convinced now that an "evil genius" has tried to seduce him. He interprets the dream as a reproach for his sins, falls asleep, and dreams of the "goods and evils" of his life, only to be awakened by a thunderclap. In the third of his dreams, Descartes discovers two books on his desk, a certain *Dictionary* and a *Corpus omnium veterum poetarum Latinorum*. Looking into the book of Latin poetry he falls upon the line *Quod vitae sectabor iter*, "What road shall I follow in life?" Suddenly a stranger appears, citing a line beginning *Est et non*, which Descartes then tries to find in the anthology on the table. Unable to do so, he tells the stranger of another verse by Aussonius beginning *Quod vitae sectabor iter*, but is again unable to find the page before the stranger disappears.

Still sleeping, Descartes dreams an interpretation of the

dreams he has just had: "[He judged] that the *Dictionary* wanted to say [nothing other than] all the sciences collected together; and that the [collection of poems] . . . showed in particular and in a more particular manner Philosophy and Wisdom [*Sagesse*] conjoined." He further considers that even trifling poets often express thoughts which are more "serious" and "sensitive" than natural philosophers, who have only reason to assist them, because they have been filled with "the divinity of Enthusiasm" and the "power of the Imagination."

> By the poets assembled in the *Anthology* he understood Revelation and the Enthusiasm that, he made bold to hope, would continue to single him out. The piece *Est et Non*, which is the *Yes and No* of Pythagoras, he understood to be the Truth and Falsity in all human knowledge and the profane sciences. . . . Seeing that all these things worked out so well with his inclinations, he was bold enough to convince himself that it was the Spirit of Truth that had wanted to open to him the treasures of all the sciences in this dream.

The origins of Cartesianism, the arising of modern science, are to be found, Descartes himself insisted, in a dream in which the powers of Enthusiasm and Imagination open "the treasures of all the sciences."

One could conclude that Wordsworth's "philosophic Friend" was Descartes himself, who appears in the retold dream both in the guise of Don Quixote, to suggest the dream-inspired, the "quixotic" quest of science, and in the guise of an Arab, to recall the people who conserved the classical heritage and brought numbers, and more importantly, zero, to Europe. And just as such oppositions are overcome, so in the course of his poetic career the dream of Descartes becomes the dream of Wordsworth. The stone of geometric truth is furrowed and hollowed by the poetic imagination to form a prophetic shell: in this way cosmic certainties of geometric truth underwrite apocalyptic intimations of the divine nature of imagination. This shell of poetic prophecy, drawing the poet and the geometrician into the same spiral of associations, thus both conserves Descartes's dream and sounds Wordsworth's poetic vocation:

> Imagination! lifting up itself
> Before the eye and progress of my Song
> Like an unfather'd vapour; here that Power,
> In all the might of its endowments, came
> Athwart me; I was lost as in a cloud,
> Halted, without struggle to break through.
> And now recovering, to my Soul I say
> I recognise thy glory; in such strength
> Of usurpation, in such visitings
> Of awful promise, when the light of sense
> Goes out in flashes that have shewn to us
> The invisible world.[4]

For Wordsworth as for Descartes, the vocations of science and poetry are literally a "calling" that follows in the archetypal pattern of conversion. Descartes's path to science begins in the whirl of an opposing wind, thus forming a *via negativa* upon which certitude can be achieved only through a profound doubt. Science can only be inspired by Imagination. And Wordsworth's own poetic autobiography can arrive at its ultimate annunciation by assuming the dream of Descartes and retranslating it into the language of prophecy.

How, after all, does a mind "grow" out of nature? What is its relationship to its brain? What is that brain's relationship to its skull and to other encapsulated organisms like seeds or like molluscs which live in shells? What relationship does a seashell have with a stone, and what relationship does a book have with both? Wordsworth may have worried about the fate of a frail book in a living world, but his dream suggests that one can find books in natural forms, that the memory of the natural world, both the great waters of the first and the last deluge, are conserved within the curves of a shell. The dream-work would appear to speak the nonsensical language of pure metaphor, but that is only because we cannot quite imagine how a stone or a shell could convey anything but an analogy of meaning, a "symbol"—a fragment that is completed when its lost half is joined to it—of a larger meaning it only rhetorically signifies. The merely "literary" constructions we place on metaphor and symbol and allegory convince us that such natural tropes are only resemblances, similitudes, ghostly familiars.

In his *Vues philosophiques de la gradation naturelle des formes de l'être, ou les essais de la nature qui apprend à faire homme* (1786), J. B. Robinet offered an early theory of evolution which relies not on accidental mutations leading to the assimilation of advantageous form, but on a personification of nature as an artist. Gaston Bachelard writes that Robinet's book describes and illustrates

> Lithocardites (heart stones), Encephalites (which are a prelude to the brain), stones that imitate a jaw-bone, the foot, the kidney, the ear, the eye, the hand, muscles—then Orchis, Diorchis, Triorchis, the Prialopites, Colites Phalloids, which imitate the male organs, and Histerpetia, which imitate the female organs. . . . It would be a mistake to see nothing in this but a reference to language habits that name new objects by comparing them with other commonplace ones. Here names think and dream, the imagination is active. Lithocardites are heart shells, rough draughts of a heart that one day will beat. . . . Shells, like fossils, are so many attempts on the part of nature to prepare forms of the different parts of the human body; they are bits of man and bits of woman. In fact Robinet gives a description of the Conch of Venus that represents a woman's vulva.[5]

Explaining this last identification, Robinet writes, "We should not be surprised at the assiduity with which Nature has multiplied models of the generative organs, in view of the importance of these organs."

And like a shell, the complex exterior of an ear, a mouth, or a vulva infolds across lips, past an epithelial sleekness, into a fluid, sea-like realm of metabolic tides and circulations. Brain, stomach, womb: these are the chambers where sound waves, food, and semen are joined and translated into sound, energy, and life. Encountered on a stretch of sand, like any pyramid, the castaway shell and its deserted chambers seem at first only an empty tomb, but it is, more importantly, a sign of a life and an architecture we cannot explain. How could the earliest Pharaohs have *begun* with ancient Egypt's most accomplished architectural feats? And how is it and why is it that a spineless gastropod responding to the laws of survival should be able to develop a carapace of such perfection that it seems the outgrowth of both mathematical and aesthetic calculation? Placed to the ear, the seashell only sounds its own absence and death by returning the body's own tides to itself.

A certain *Coralliophila pyriformis* Kira, found in the coral reefs of Japanese waters, presents a striking three-dimensional view of vulva, labia, and womb such as one encounters in an anatomical plate. And yet these opening labia can also suggest an orchid awaiting the thorax of a bee able to bear its pollen to other orchids gesturing from other trees. Or consider the *Terebra praelongas* Deshayes, or indeed any other species of the genus *Terebra*: these slender spirals, known as auger shells because of their drill-like shape, may adorn the sands of shallow, tropical waters, but they can also be found between the eyes of the unicorns capering in the narrow corrals of medieval tapestries. And Aphrodite arises, immaculate and mature, from half of a great scallop, a divine, virgin pearl of great price. All of this is to say that the shell has the structure of a living metaphor able to move from the notional realm of imagination to the hard and durable realm of organic form.

"Like a pure sound or a melodic system of pure sounds in the midst of noises," Valéry writes, "so a *crystal*, a *flower*, a *seashell* stand out from the common disorder of perceptible things." And they stand out for the simple reason that their forms signify a larger order absent in perceptible "things," the form of an art practiced by what modern science has imagined to be "chance" itself. Our astonishment at such organization, far from being diminished by the laws of evolution, can only be augmented by our first intellectual reaction, which is to find chance in the face of evident design. By abandoning the image of nature as artisan, as a tireless draftsman whose sketches litter the beaches and deserts of the world, scientific culture must accept then an even uncannier artificer: chance itself, which finds in the most unpromising elements the necessary vocabulary and syntax for an order, such as one finds in the chambered nautilus, *Nautilus pompilius* Linne. This masterpiece may be governed by the immediate laws of molecular structure, but not by any other demands than survival, which can only be met by chance mutations. And of this shell, like the Great Pyramid, one can ask: what is it to say that chance or design, lost arts or genius are responsible for these memorials? Valéry writes,

> The problem after all is no more futile nor any more naive than speculation about *who made* a certain fine work in music or poetry; whether it was born of the Muse, or sent by Fortune, or whether it was the fruit of long labor. To say that someone composed it, that his name was Mozart or Virgil, is not to say much; a statement of this sort is lifeless, for the creative spirit in us bears no name.[6]

And such names as we offer in explanation are themselves nothing but metaphors. Names like Mozart and Virgil, words like Muse and Fortune and Chance, indicate only what we do not understand.

In this last instance the piety of scientists can readily be observed: for it is under this veil of chance—the muse of modern biology—that they conceal their sense, more profound than any layman's, of the infinite artistry evident in the simplest— as in the most remarkable—of seashells. For naturalists have long realized that a nautilus's spiraling shell, and other natural architectures, display examples of the ratio 1.61803 to 1, which, since at least the Renaissance, has been called the Golden Section. The Golden Section, which is displayed serially in the so-called Fibonacci series of numbers (wherein each is the sum of the previous two numbers), not only describes the precise way in which the spiraling shell turns, but it also describes aspects of the Great Pyramid, the Parthenon, and other monumental structures from antiquity to Le Corbusier.[7] A critic has even claimed to have found elaborations on the proportion in the structure of Virgil's *Aeneid*.[8] And a Fibonacci Society was founded in California in the early sixties to trace evidence for the "thinking" which reaches from a seashell, via the Great Pyramid, to the poetry of Virgil, and beyond.

In the early years of this century the elegant and erudite scientist D'Arcy Wentworth Thompson argued in his *Growth and Form* that "there cannot be a physical or dynamical, though there may well be a mathematical *law of growth* which is common to, and which defines, the spiral form in *Nautilus*, in

*Globigerina,* in the ram's horn, and in the inflorescence of the sunflower. Nature at least exhibits in them all *'un reflet des formes rigoreuses qu'étudie la géométrie.'* " Wordsworth's stone and shell are thus, perhaps, less opposite than complementary, a dream vision of the consonance of inorganic and organic form, of geometry and poetry, of the dead stone of the earth and the living mind of nature. Where, then, does "the growth of a poet's mind" described in *The Prelude* begin if not in natural forms? People have from the beginning established such correspondences between the human body and the living and nonliving world through myth and poetry.

If the shell is the link between the stone and the ear, the earth and the vulva, the whirpool and the mind, chance and design—if the shell, in other words, is a metaphor of a larger metaphoric process of organic development, it is within its spiral we must turn and turn and turn. For a spiral is a compromise between the progressive element of the line and the recursive, conservative disposition of a circle. A spiral, like a metaphor, is a category of trope (*tropos,* turn): each "new" development in a spiral is both a departure and a return to its own nature. Seen in this light all nature is governed by a certain spiral and metaphoric logic. Myth and poetry prepare the way for geometric description by establishing a world governed by correspondences, similitudes that reveal the repetition and elaboration of certain forms. Of all these recurring metaphoric and geometric forms, the spiral would appear the most promising, if not the most prophetic. D'Arcy Thompson writes,

> In the growth of a shell we can conceive no simpler law than this, namely, that it shall widen and lengthen in the same unvarying proportions: and this simplest of laws is that which Nature tends to follow. The shell, like the creature within it, grows in size *but does not change its shape;* and the existence of this constant relativity of growth, or constant similarity of form, is of the essence, and may be made the basis of a definition, of the equiangular spiral.

But what function can such form have in an evolutionary scheme which only rewards survival, not ingenuity and perfection? Thompson continues:

We find the same forms which (save for external ornament) are mathematically identical, repeating themselves in all periods in the world's geological history; and we see them mixed up, one with another, irrespective of climate or local conditions, in the depths and on the shores of every sea. It is hard indeed (to my mind) to see in such a case as this where Natural Selection necessarily enters in.[9]

What clearly does enter in is an innate disposition toward forms which can be described geometrically. The Belousov-Zhabotinsky reaction discovered in 1958, initiated by the combination of inorganic elements, is characterized by the formation of perfectly concentric circles and interconnected spiral "cells."[10] Such reactions are sometimes referred to as "self-organizing," although doubtless no one using this phrase means that any "self" is involved. But what is the difference between our ordinary sense of a "self" (with consciousness, motives, and intentions) and the reflexivity implied by the phrases *"self*-organizing reactions" or *"auto*-poetic form?"

The spiral appears to be a kind of formalized nostalgia which links our geometry with the galaxies, the solar system, the pattern of our major internal organs (beginning with the heart), the figure of the univalve shell, the Belousov-Zhabotinsky spirals, not to mention whirlpools, whirlwinds, and the spiral etchings which can be found in burial vaults in neolithic Europe, from Malta to Britain.

According to Michel Serres and Ilya Prigogine, we may turn to Lucretius for an account of the momentous occurrence that begins with the first twist and turn, the first swerve (*Clinamen*) in the flow of atoms. Lucretius writes:

When the atoms are travelling straight down through empty space by their own weight, at quite indeterminate times and places they swerve ever so little from their course, just so much that you can call it a change of direction. If it were not for this swerve, everything would fall downwards like rain-drops through the abyss of space. No collision would take place and no impact of atom on atom would be created. Thus nature would never have created anything.[11]

Natural poetry, like its verbal derivatives, begins with a fecund deviation, a chance turning aside, from which every subsequent formation develops. In the beginning—one can hear the seashell incanting—was the trope.

For Ovid, as for Lucretius, the world of discrete objects is only an illusion of ordinary vision: beneath the serene surfaces of a meadow, a bush, a stone, or a shell is a constantly flowing current of interweaving relationship. But where Lucretius saw the fundamental aspect in the face of indissoluble atoms, Ovid sees in forms the traces of the natural history of women and gods, goddesses and men, animals and plants, stars and mountains. The world, for Ovid, is an ongoing narrative of bodies passing between forms, a metamorphic world that the metaphoric language of the poet deciphers and yet perpetuates. The anatomy of the shellfish or the spider, the structure of the finger or the measure of a line of poetry are all aspects of this proto-ecology unveiled by the stories of metamorphoses. If the blood of Adonis can become the anemone, this is because his beauty and his death do not—cannot—simply pass into nothingness. They must leave a trace. If Arachne can become a spider, this is because all natural forms reveal, through myth and metaphor, their lines of descent and kinship. Character, both psychological and anatomical, is a kind of inscription.

*The Metamorphoses* of Ovid are approximations of an ecology that biologists would only begin to discover after Darwin. The *logos* of the *oikos* (house, habitat), ecology began as a metaphoric display of connections revealed by the poetic necessity of discovering or imposing semblances, and so kinship. In the time of Linnaeus, these relationships were conceived as changeless and undynamic: the grids of the natural historian's tables had fallen across living forms like a net. Beneath and within these nets, Darwin discovered, like Ovid, a differential narrative and a different imagery: he saw evidence for a sublime story of an older earth and an evolution of forms—that is to say the continuous metamorphoses of a living world. Between modern biology and ancient mythology there is an implicit link that one can discover in the anatomy of the hand and the measure of a line of poetry.

School children were once taught that the metrical foot of

a dactyl was, strangely enough, like a finger: it began with a long or stressed syllable and was followed by two unstressed syllables, like the shorter bones completing the finger. There is, then, this beautiful symmetry between the anatomy of the *dáktŭlos* and the structure of the *dactyl*: /– –. These children were also told that the anapest meant a "reversed" dactyl (– –/), that the spondee's two stresses were a "libation," and that the trochee (/–), meaning "running," galloped like a horse. They may have been taught that these mnemonic devices were also etymologies, and that these etymologies told the story of an age before writing, when even the bones of one's fingers could be relied upon to carry a line of poetry, as a line of poetry carried a story, and a story a world. The Homeric epics are articulated by these joints in language, epithets like "rosy-fingered dawn"—*rododáctŭlos éos*—which figured sunrise at sea through metaphors of rose petals, fingers, and Homer's own dactylic hexameter. Add to this story the conventional blindness of Homer and one can picture a poet counting his verses, long before they were written down, on the bones in his hand. Discounting the thumb, a line of Homer can be counted twice on one hand, or once on both. The "rosy-fingered dawn" epithet which turns up throughout the Homeric poems is thus doubly-articulated, and so can indicate the red petals of sun refracted through a moist atmosphere and a dawning in the West of a poetic meter whose perfection appears out of nowhere—unless one imagines that poetry *begins* with the skeleton.

Gregory Bateson has made the argument that we have neglected this metaphoric and narrative aspect of living forms. Thinking of such literary matters as secondary, technical kinds of representation, we ignore the fact that all organisms are, given their finite life spans, their origin and their progeny, representations, narratives, and tropes themselves. According to the central dogma of genetics, evolution itself is directed by tropes, turns, or mutations away from the actual and prosaic replication of a genetic code. But since the code is itself a creation of successful tropes—so the dogma holds—one would also have to recognize that the rule of evolution is metaphoric, and the metaphoric aspects of organisms are unfolded within the grand narratives of evolution. But Bateson would go even further and argue that the intrinsic order of a single organism is itself structured like a narrative and that, necessarily, cultural narratives are elaborations on organistic patterns.[12] Just as the skeleton of a human hand, forearm, and upper arm can be seen by analogy in other mammals, such as a horse, so fundamental human myths—the Osiris and Demeter cycles—can be traced to the narratives of the sun and the seasons. When Aristotle insisted that a tragedy must have a beginning, a middle, and an end, he only adapted the evident teleology of a single life, a year, or a day. And the tragic aspect depends on a transmutation of this narrative before the inevitable return of the beginning.

The literary, which is to say the unsettling aspect, of a shell or a skeleton is that it continues to exist after life has passed from it. Within the fleshy narrative of character and personality there is a plot like a stone, a pattern which links all men and women to the generic and the mortal. Thus even more uncanny is a seashell abandoned on the edge of the sea, and later found on a mountain miles above it.

It was thus that Darwin, during his voyage on the *Beagle*, began to imagine the dynamic and ancient nature of the earth. While climbing in the Andes, some miles above the Pacific, he discovered the fossils of seashells:

> Even at the very crest of the Peuquenes, at the height of 13,210 feet, and above it, the black clay-slate contained numerous marine remains, amongst which a gryphaea is the most abundant, likewise shells, resembling turritellae, terebratulae, and an ammonite. It is an old story, but not the less wonderful, to hear of shells, which formerly were crawling about at the bottom of the sea, being now elevated nearly 14,000 feet above its level.[13]

Later he would imagine, like Wordsworth, the connection between the animate and the inanimate. And later still another Englishman and gentleman scientist, James Lovelock, would propose that the earth itself, considering its energy and history of movement, was a kind of organism and would rename it, following the suggestion of William Golding, "Gaia."[14]

The seashell, having become relatively speaking a permanent remainder of a life, establishes the nature and function of poetic immortality. The poems of Wordsworth or Milton, or of any prophetic or sublime work of art, assume the effect and cosmic resonance of this discovered shell. And thus one can see the ways in which organisms, myths, and texts are all elaborated from the same narrative, and narrative is always a form of recall, of recollection, of memory.

Scientists such as Ilya Prigogine and Erich Jantsch have argued that organic structures do indeed "begin" with the spiral or turbulent movement in fluid media such as water or air, which either deepen into a vortex or rise into a cone. There is thus a passageway from the world of stars and seas, stones and water to the world of living creatures. For Jantsch, evolution is *auto-poeisis*, a self-making of the kind described in *The Prelude*.[15] It is only by constantly moving away from a center that such instances of chaos retain their forms as what Prigogine calls "dissipative structures." Whether one inspects the turbulence in a stream caused by a stone, or views a drop of water falling in a brimming bowl which raises a corona-like splash, or inspects the curvatures of shell or horn, or observes the spiraling diamonds on the face of a sunflower, one discovers this startling complicity of life and geometry, of mathematical description and poetic forms: a seashell is both evidence and metaphor for this necessary relationship.

# 6

## The Memory of Nature

The lord whose oracle is at Delphi neither speaks nor conceals, but gives signs.

—Heraclitus

Long before its lord was recognized to be Apollo, Delphi on the southern slopes of Mount Parnassus had been the site of a pre-Hellenic, chthonic deity. It is thus difficult to know whether Heraclitus, in the above quote, meant that mysterious underground forces or the god of light and reason speaks in signs. But it is easy enough to realize that it is the Apollonian voice that speaks in us when we consider questions such as this, which presume that there must be a clear-cut difference, rather than a necessary relationship, between opposites. Metamorphic mythologies, by contrast, usually show the whole world as a close texture of signs in which human desire and fate can be read—and into which specific human desires and fates are continually being written.

If a windflower arouses in us a vague yet undeniable response, a myth explains that we are in a sense recalling, and so feeling, the fate of Adonis whose blood blossomed in the anemone. Myths of metamorphosis are thus not only first drafts of a general evolutionary theory of life, they provide an explanation of why we feel anything for a flower, a shell, or a star. The apparent naiveté of myths conceals an unconscious recognition that the world is, as Baudelaire recognized, a vast system of correspondences wherein we discover aspects of our own mind. Just as the mind finds expression in a meadow, a seashore, or the sky, so too a flower, a shell, and a star find expression in the human mind. The mythic sign always reveals a human face.

Since Sir Francis Bacon and Descartes, modern science has defined itself in opposition to mythology, seeking to discipline and reduce the metaphoric nature of signs, and aspiring to achieve an unequivocal description of what the world is. Science thus has turned away from the mythic insight that all acts of perception are metamorphic. Where mythologies constantly narrate the desires, conflicts, deaths, births, and metamorphoses of men and women in a world of clouds, rivers, trees, birds, and seas, scientific narratives concern "movement," "development," "behavior," and "formation"; "matter," "organisms," "environments," and "species." This scientific scheme of generic entities is no less mythological, but it has become "reality"—which is to say, it has become unequivocal and inescapable, our modern fate.

Thus the molecular model of DNA first constructed at Cambridge University's Cavendish Laboratory in 1953 has become, like the model of the atom constructed by Niels Bohr, one of the central emblems of modern science, as well as a charmed image of what a human being *fundamentally* is. The double helix and the atomic model based on the solar system, like devices taken from a medieval alchemical treatise, have both descriptive and symbolic aspects. A microcosm superimposed upon a macrocosm, the atomic model hints at nuclear apocalypse, while the double helix suggests the spiral staircase of evolution, the elegant and symmetrical attraction which transforms nonliving elements into the rudiments of life.

The archetypal character of these two scientific developments derives from an ancient tradition of interpreting and reducing nature to first principles, mythic emblems, and powerful formulae. $E = mc^2$, the atomic model, the double helix have entered into the iconography of the age because they draw upon these prescientific means of understanding nature by putting in its place a kind of charmed model or double. The making of models, the telling of stories, and the mathematical expression of the intrinsic relations between human numbers are all responses to this fundamental need to understand nature by reducing it to an image.

Of course scientists maintain that their actions, however brilliant and laborious, do nothing other than reveal or unveil the structure of reality. Like a hero from myth going in quest of a fleece, a grail, or a ring that will bring life to his dying kingdom, the scientist is often imagined (by himself and others) as one whose intellectual and experimental activities recover only what has been lost or obscured by the ages and the contingencies of material form. As Heraclitus is reputed to have said, nature loves to hide. And genetic scientists like Jacques Monod and Richard Dawkins have, rather immodestly, claimed that the grand drama of human evolution, beginning with the first nucleic acids and recently culminating in man, arrives at its climax when scientists like themselves discover the nucleic acid—and thus the "secret of life."

In a myth, this recovery of a lost object or emblem would be followed by the return of vitality to the land: once the knight has returned with the grail, the Fisher-King's mysterious wound heals and the wasteland blooms. The genetic myth offers its own, characteristically technological, redemption: genetic engineering. Where earlier myths naively indicated that the recovery of a lost object, symbolic of our native inheritance from a universe which is whole and alive, could in itself redeem man's wasted life, Richard Dawkins explains that the discovery of the molecular component of the gene will allow people to engineer their own redemption. "Let us try to *teach* generosity and altruism because we are born selfish. Let us understand what our own selfish genes are up to, because we may then at least have the chance to upset their designs, something which no other species has ever aspired to."[1] Like one of the early Gnostics, Dawkins believes that creation itself was the fall to which we are all heir. Salvation, then, may simply be a matter of cloning those traits which a fallen nature has failed to encourage.

Genetic engineering may be a novel technical response to nature, but it follows in a tradition that leads back to the Book of Genesis. Here, as in other things, modern science has adopted the Judeo-Christian assumption that nature is a representation, a manifestation of a fundamental word, code, model, or software. Since nature is essentially the representation of an informing principle, to "know" nature is also to possess the means to control it. Here, as in the sexual aspect of imperialism, knowledge is a controlling, patriarchal force which must penetrate, inform, and reform a passive or feminine nature. Like missionaries who studied Chinese or Urdu in order to convert "natives" to Christianity, DNA researchers have from the beginning planned the improvement of nature. To understand nature, one has first to locate its fundamental and irreducible component, DNA (or the Word), and then work to transform it.

The God of Genesis brings order to the world through speech: from light to humanity, creation is but the unfolding of divine words. But within nature, another kind of ordering word is created: " 'Let the earth produce fresh growth, let there be on the earth plants bearing seed, fruit-trees bearing fruit each with seed according to its kind.' So it was; the earth yielded fresh growth, plants bearing seed according to its kind" (1.9–12). The animal world is likewise enjoined to be "fruitful and multiply" according to the metaphor of the vegetable world. Seeds and generation carry forward the original creation by containing God's words. Within this context of metaphysical and physical creation, human beings are inserted:

> "Let us make man in our image [*tselem*] and likeness [*demut*] to rule the fish in the sea, the birds of heaven, the cattle, all wild animals on earth and all reptiles that crawl upon the earth." So God created man in his own image; in the image of God he created him; male and female he created them. God blessed them and said to them, "Be fruitful and increase, fill the earth and subdue it, rule over the fish in the sea, the birds of heaven, and every living thing that moves upon the earth." And God said, "I give you all plants that bear seed everywhere on earth, and every tree bearing fruit which yields seed: they shall be yours for food."
>
> (1.27–30)

Master of the world created by God's words, Adam is himself both "image" (Heb. *tselem*, a formal representation such as a statue or icon) and "likeness" (*demut*, a general resemblance) of God, both an analog and a digital representation.

The fall of Adam and Eve could be seen, then, as the corruption of this originative, divine speech: God's images, God's likenesses, somehow are drawn away from their own assigned place in creation by the enticing and false words of the serpent. The Fall means that these two images are thrown out of the garden of ideal resemblance into the sweating and imperfect realm of history. The first sin was, then, a crime against the word of God, but it is not until book 11 of Genesis that this becomes explicit and language itself falls:

> Once upon a time all the world spoke a single language and used all the same words. As men journeyed in the east, they came upon a plain in the land of Shinar and settled there. They said to one another, "Come, let us make bricks and bake them hard"; they used bricks for stone and bitumen for mortar. "Come," they said, "let us build ourselves a city and a tower with its top in the heavens, and make a name for ourselves; or we shall be dispersed over the earth."
>
> (11. 1–5)

Like Adam and Eve, the citizens of Babel aspire beyond their fallen state and hope that a city and a tower will inscribe their identity in so visible a fashion that their name will not be lost. But the Lord God, hearing this blasphemy, decides to punish his creatures yet again for their impertinence by confusing their language and scattering them across the earth.

If we are to understand, even at the most naive level, God's actions in this episode, we must admit that He is worried that human beings have not yet become aware that there can be but one modular, paradigmatic—one *divine*—language in creation. When the Judaic version of divine relations began to penetrate the European world after the triumph of Christ, it was this lesson that led to the construction of medieval Scholasticism in Latin: only by maintaining the language of pagan Rome could the Church remain Catholic and its doctrines and theology consistent.

Thus even before the coming of modern science and mathematics, the presumption that the world could be known according to the terms of a word, a command, and a law was firmly established in Europe. When Isaac Newton began to transcribe the distant God of Genesis into the watchmaker who made the world and abandoned it, he substituted "Laws" concerning the mechanics and dynamics of nature for the Scriptures. It was in this spirit that Alexander Pope composed his epitaph intended for Sir Isaac Newton and compared him to the light God created on the first day. "Nature and nature's laws lay hid in night / God said, 'Let Newton be!' and all was light." Mathematics was entrusted with the new laws of nature, and it in turn was entrusted to a new clerisy of mathematicians and physicists. Leibniz, having invented calculus (as did Newton), foresaw the shortcomings of mathematics for all but technical problems and proposed the creation of a language of Chinese-like ideograms that could become a universal language. "We have the option of fixing significations, at least in some learned language, and of agreeing on them, so as to pull down this Tower of Babel" which the European disciplines had become.[2] Such a "Universal Symbolism" was never achieved and in its place the language of mathematics became the *de facto* universal symbolism of the European sciences.

Contemporary with the beginnings of modern science in the Renaissance was another, and less successful, search for the original or fundamental language of nature. Jacob Boehme claimed that a *lingua adamica* could be recovered through what might be defined as etymological alchemy. Within all languages a devoted adept could, with the aid of interpretative devices and mystical insight, discover the original Hebrew spoken by Adam when he named the animals. The truth of Genesis could be found even in the language of the pagans, and in this way their own mythological and religious scriptures preserved the ore of divine truth.[3]

The mystical and scholarly quests for a *lingua adamica* were motivated by the basic mythic assumption that truth and wholeness are the fundamental qualities of life and that man's salvation requires that he recognize his divine birthright. The scientific and mathematical researches which led to modern physics and molecular biology assumed only that the truth of nature was to be found in the most irreducible of elements and the most irreducible expressions of those elements. Despite their enormous successes, nuclear physicists produced a strangely contradictory commentary on the scientific project which began with Newton: their technical achievements were obvious enough, but their intellectual and philosophic results did not tally at all with the materialist presumptions of science. Instead of advancing the classical idea of the cumulative nature of knowledge, the inventors of quantum physics questioned the epistemological foundations of science.

These events meant that the research into the molecular structure of DNA would carry on the highest—which is to say the most reductive—aspirations of science. Long before James D. Watson and Francis Crick had completed their famous model, it was already determined that the genetic material in cells must contain the "secret" or "code" or "language" of life.[4] Rejecting the idea that all human forms are encapsulated within the sexual element of their predecessors, Charles Darwin had posited the existence of "gemmules" whose combination provided the collective traits of the self-dividing embryo. The shift from the model of reproduction by analog to reproduction by digitalized bytes of information would have obvious appeal in the age of computers. Later students of the new science which Willam Bateson named "Genetics" worked on the potential structure of such "gemmules."[5] August Weissmann referred to "germ plasm," which performed the required reproductive function, but he insisted that each cell would require its own unique plasm if its development were to be properly guided.[6] By the 1940s scientists had decided that DNA (deoxyribonucleic acid) was the prime carrier of genetic information. One of them, Oswald Avery, foresaw even then the possibility of controlling and modifying this molecule as a means of altering the development of organisms.[7]

In other words, before anything like actual empirical evidence for the "gene" in the guise of gemmules, germ plasm, chromosomes, or DNA had been gathered, scientists had determined what it must do and also what could be done with it. Perhaps the most significant of these actions was simply to define it, since a gene is a length of the DNA molecule associated, more or less, with a certain observable trait. In contrast with palpable and definitive cellular bodies, the gene is, then, an artifact which naturalizes socialized categories of classification. The DNA molecule which formed the basis of the gene was constituted as the language of life even before its structure had been discovered. Not only was it thought to carry inherited characteristics, it was assumed to possess the information which guides the development of the embryo and the growth and functioning of the body. Evident in this speculation was a strangely reflexive logic. Once scientists had determined what the DNA must be and what it must do, they began to imagine how it could be changed to do something else—before even its rudimentary structure was known. Such thinking muted any doubts that DNA performed these functions. Scientific presumption was masked by praise for the "beauty" of the self-replicating molecule and the "miracle" that "life" could so competently employ the programming logic of the new sciences of computing, information, and artificial intelligence.

James D. Watson's best-selling account of his work with Francis Crick, *The Double Helix*, reveals how understanding the structure of DNA was as good as understanding "life itself." "Then DNA was a mystery, up for grabs, and no one was sure who would get it and whether he would deserve it if it proved as exciting as we semisecretly believed." Besides being a "mystery," DNA was also variously, Watson writes, a "Rosetta stone for unravelling the true secret of life," a "key" to understanding how parental traits are inherited, "the secret of the gene," "the key to the secret of life," and "the most golden of all molecules." Drawing on the traditions of Egyptology, cryptography, and conquest, Watson wonders who will "crack DNA," advises a colleague that "DNA could fall," and worries how to "win the DNA structure."

The interpretation of the meaning of DNA, quite apart from the complex and ingenious discovery of its structure, was guided by the melodramatic logic which required that the "mystery" of DNA would become, once it was described, the "key" to life. The more the molecule was styled a "secret" (held by whom? entrusted by whom? and for what purpose?) the more its structure would mean.[8] It was rather like believing that learning how bricks (or proteins) were produced was the same as knowing the art of architecture.

The classic article written by Watson and Crick in 1953 to

announce their discovery was free of the melodramatic imagery of gene sleuthing from Watson's later "personal account of the discovery of the structure of DNA." Erwin Chargaff, one of the authorities cited in its notes, describes it this way:

> The tone was certainly unusual: somehow oracular and imperious, almost decalogous. Difficulties, such as the even now [1973] not well-understood manner of unwinding the huge bi-helical structures under the conditions of the living cell, were brushed aside, in a Mr. Fix-It spirit that was later to become so evident in our scientific literature. . . . I could see that this was the dawn of something new: a sort of normative biology that commanded nature to behave in accordance with the models.[9]

Chargaff saw in the article not only the dawn of a new age of model-building (which in the decades after World War II would also include structuralist linguistics, anthropology, psychoanalysis, literary criticism, as well as the systemic or cybernetic theories of computing, biology, and society), but also the return of the idea of the scientist as patriarchal law-giver, a prerogative which modern physicists had to give up when they explored the subatomic realm.

In this spirit, molecular biology took up the standard of fundamental science by presuming that to understand the structure of what was thought to be fundamental was equivalent to understanding the whole. Thus Watson recalls the moment when he proposed the basic tenet of what is commonly called the "Central Dogma" of genetic microbiology: "On the wall above my desk I taped up a paper sheet saying DNA > RNA > protein. The arrows did not signify chemical transformations, but instead expressed the transfer of genetic information from the sequences of nucleotides in DNA molecules to the sequences of amino acids in proteins."[10] The Central Dogma maintains that this sequence is irreversible and that DNA is the source of all "information" leading to the construction of proteins—and thus to "life itself." The Mosaic nature of this thinking extended from the tone of the articles of Watson and Crick to the dictatorial role of DNA within the cell. A rather odd identification was established between this most golden of molecules and this most golden of new sciences:

molecular biology, it appeared, needed DNA almost as much as "life" did.

From such an advantageous position, molecular biologists began in subsequent decades to enjoy the authority which accrues to those who have sounded the mystery of life. Jacques Monod was able to draw something like an entire philosophy from his work with DNA and RNA. Where structuralists in other fields of French intellectual life turned their backs on existentialism, seeing it as an overly personal and unnecessary set of inferences, Monod directly linked his work on nucleic acids with perennial philosophic questions, even to the point of citing Camus's "The Myth of Sisyphus" as an epigraph. From his vantage point of scientific expertise, Monod explained the ramifications of molecular biology for the entire "project" of human evolution:

> The origin and lineage of the whole biosphere are reflected in the ontogenesis of a functional protein. And the ultimate source of the project that living beings present, pursue, and accomplish is revealed in this message—in this neat, exact, but essentially indecipherable text formed by primary structure. Indecipherable, since before expressing the physiologically necessary function which it performs spontaneously, it discloses nothing in its structure other than the pure chance of its origin. But for us, this truly is the more profound meaning of this message which comes to us from the most distant reaches of time.[11]

Monod confuses the categories of his chosen field of study, molecular biology, with "the origin and lineage of the whole biosphere" and "the ultimate source of the project that living beings represent." Identifying what are considered the most elementary physical properties with philosophical or metaphysical principles such as "origin" and "source," Monod translates the technical study of acids, proteins, and enzymes into philosophic reflection. Monod is thus encouraged to claim that the "message" of molecular structure is both indecipherable and completely legible, because he has taken its opacity as an emblem for a world based on chance. Just in this way banal existentialism transforms the supposed "absurdity" of existence, the "meaninglessness" of life, into a metaphysical revelation: "If he accepts this message in its full significance, man must at last wake out of his millenary dream and discover his total solitude, his fundamental isolation. He must realize that, like a gypsy, he lives on the boundary of an alien world; a world that is deaf to his music, and as indifferent to his hopes as it is to his sufferings or his crimes." Once Monod has tied humanity and the whole of life to the "functional protein" at its "origin" in order to establish the authority of his philosophic reflections, he cuts that line. Not only does "man" lose his rapport with the living world, but Monod cuts himself loose from his own authority.

By contrast, Richard Dawkins's cheerful exposition of "selfish genes" would appear part of the brave new world of genetic transformations. Dawkins believes that his discipline has "solved" the "mystery" of man's existence. "We are all survival machines for the same kind of replicator-molecules called DNA—but there are many different ways of making a living in the world, and the replicators have built a vast range of mechanisms to exploit."[12] The "mystery" of life proves not to have been very mysterious after all: it happens to be very much like advanced industrial culture. For Dawkins, there is no fundamental difference between a gene and a human being.

It is not at all surprising that this mystery should have been solved by Darwin and Wallace during the first half-century after the appearance of capitalist culture. Dawkins, it should be mentioned, is sensitive to this point, and chastizes those who confuse describing a phenomenon with endorsing it. Dawkins may protest that he is simply and objectively representing the activities of genes, but he also admits, necessarily, that his calling genes "selfish" is in effect a "thought experiment," a metaphor to illustrate the difficult-to-explain relationship between blind chance and iron necessity, the world of a "blind watchmaker." By his account, then, the selfish and competitive gene is a figure of speech, but one for which he has not had far to search. Once the complexities of the subject have been conveniently interpreted in this manner, confirmation of the thesis is no less difficult to find: one has only to drive a car in urban traffic to recognize its supposed truth.

Scientists talk about "doing science," because they recognize that science is, strictly speaking, a highly controlled activity in which certain results are obtained. Interpreting such findings cannot, however, become a subject for scientific reflection. Those findings can either encourage other experiments which may in turn influence the way other experiments are conducted, or they may lead to certain technical products. The advantage of technical applications is obvious: if one can produce a marketable product, thinking about it is not necessary. Thinking about the findings is left to those willing to illustrate and make accessible difficult procedures and often unarticulated assumptions, or to the eminent and reflective elder scientist who has given up active research. In both cases, it is no longer "science." This is not to say that hard-working scientists who do not indulge in such activities can avoid these problems: it is simply easier to act as if they do not exist.

Watson, Monod, and Dawkins all share the basically Judeo-Christian-Cartesian notion that nature is an enormous artifact governed by some privileged and internalized program: the God of Genesis, the *res cogitans* of Descartes, the code of Watson, the message of Monod, and the gene of Dawkins are all part of the same heritage. And in the sociobiology imagined by E. O. Wilson, even original sin, in the guise of various antisocial genes, has been revived. Despite the dramatic emergence of modern science from the domination of the Church, there are fewer differences in the way each envisions nature than one might think. Jean Baudrillard, the French social theorist and critic of structuralism, has pointed out the ways in which the conceptualization and reception of DNA was governed by such a tradition. Commenting on Monod's *Chance and Necessity*, he observes

> a nature distorted by fantasy like she always was, metaphysical sanctuary no longer of origin and substance, but this time of the code; the code must have an "objective" basis. What could be better for that purpose than the molecule and genetics? Monod is the strict theologian of this molecular transcendence, Edgar Morin the rapt disciple (A.D.N. [French, *Acide deoxyribonucleide*, DNA] + Adonai!).[13]

The chance pun in French between Adonai, or Lord, and ADN

succinctly, even necessarily, explains the authority and appeal of this Central Dogma of genetics: a general explanatory principle unburdened by metaphysics. As Dawkins happily admits, "DNA works in mysterious ways."

By referring to the code or the "language of life," geneticists have the benefit of a metaphysical explanation without paying for it in "scientific credibility." In doing so, they have re-commenced the labors of the alchemists, the mystic philologists, and the physicists: the repair of Babel. But unlike their predecessors, they have sought not merely to uncover the *Ursprache* of nature but to change both language and nature to suit their own designs. As the God of Genesis foresaw, "henceforth nothing they have in mind to do will be beyond their reach." In the spirit of the builders of Babel, they plan to mount to a kind of technological paradise of rectified organic designs on the sinuous ladder of DNA.

T. S. Kuhn maintains that, when a scientific paradigm becomes accepted, a period of arduous labor follows during which its assumptions produce a vast body of literature in support of the paradigm. Kuhn calls such work "normal science" because it is basically devoted to "puzzle-solving" or demonstrating the validity of the paradigm when applied to new areas of research. Gradually, however, data may be produced which seems to depart from the most commonly-held views. Such anomalous findings, when they appear frequently, may lead a scientific community into a period of crisis out of which a new paradigm may well emerge.

The crisis in the neo-Darwinian paradigm is less evident than it might be because so much of the research is focused on modifying the functions of DNA rather than modifying conceptual models. But these flaws have become more and more evident in the last decade. In a 1988 article for *Scientific American*, Joan Argetsinger Steitz shows how certain small nuclear ribonucleoproteins (SNURPS) help to edit out meaningless strips of DNA (introns).[14] "The picture of snRNP's working in concert in the spliceosomes suggest nothing if not a well-oiled machine," she writes, offering one of the least-examined of scientific metaphors. Focused completely on the technical description of how SNURPS and spliceosomes work to delete introns and splice exons, Steitz's article relies heavily on passive voice descriptions of how the molecule "is edited"; how DNA sequences "are described"; how the primary transcript "is littered with segments of genetic nonsense"; how most of the RNA "becomes degraded"; and how certain parts of the pre-mRNA "were targeted for degradation." DNA, once an organic equivalent of the Logos, can be "more intron than exon."

Grammar is rarely used to question the conclusions of scientists, but certainly these phrases make one thing clear: scientists allude to a hidden or occult principle in such passive voice constructions. The initial and heroic talk of authoritative "codes" and "keys" has been overtaken by the imagery of "proofreading," "editing," and "deletion." The question, of course, is what agency is involved in this editing. It is like trying to imagine who or what sees what the eye focuses, the retina codes, and the brain uncodes.

In other articles from 1988 two separate teams provided evidence, since contested, that there may be some truth to the old Larmarckian heresy that organisms can pass on acquired characteristics. In the journal *Cell*, Janet Shaw, Jean Feagin, Larry Simpson, and Kenneth Stuart describe something inside the cell that appears to alter the genetic information, sometimes by as much as sixty percent.[15] And John Cairns, Julie Overbaugh, and Stephan Miller in *Nature* report data showing that certain bacteria appear to direct their own mutations in order to adapt to their environment.[16] Reviewing the conflicts between what they call "reductionists" and "romantics," Cairns et al seem reluctant to join those "romantics" who see the evolution "as just another manifestation of the mysteriousness of living things." But they also write, "when we come to consider what mechanism might be the basis for the forms of mutation described in this paper we find that molecular biology has, in the interim, deserted the reductionist. Now, almost anything seems possible."

One begins to wonder if DNA—as a principle of general biological explanation—is not only an emblem of scientific hubris, but simply a myth, similar to the philosopher's stone, the *lingua adamica*, and the doctrine which held that God had inscribed his signature in the living world. If one reads carefully one may notice a certain tentativeness when its champions speak of the way in which DNA guides, not only the formation of amino acids which compose protein, but the development of a body in the womb and its subsequent growth outside of it. Monod writes, with some bravado, "It is perfectly true that embryonic development is in appearance one of the most miraculous phenomena in the whole of biology. It is also true that these phenomena, admirably described by embryologists, continue in large part (for technical reasons) to elude genetic and biochemical analysis, which alone could lead to an understanding of them."[17] Given the fact that geneticists only have some knowledge of how DNA directs the formation of certain proteins and have been able through engineering to alter the nature of such productions, these are bold claims. The formation of proteins is one thing; directing the formation of a complete, living child is another. Dawkins is no less sanguine, but is less generous to his fellow scientists: "[DNA] indirectly supervises the manufacture of a different kind of molecule—protein. Exactly how this eventually leads to the development of a body is a story which will take decades, perhaps centuries, for embryologists to work out. But it is a fact that it does."[18] In a field where neither money nor time is in short supply, defenders may allow centuries to work out the technicalities which stand between monitoring and interfering with protein production and a complete biochemical understanding of epigenesis. The Human Genome Project organized by James Watson, even if it manages to provide a complete map of the genetic composition, would only provide, like a concordance to the works of Homer or Virgil, the elements for such an understanding.

According to Erwin Chargaff, the pervasiveness of the first heady but persistent claims for DNA is intimately connected with the narrowness of its scientific foundation. Chargaff believes that too often the single bacterium *Escherichia coli* "impersonates nature" in the conclusions drawn by researchers for the simple reason that it is amenable to manipulation and observation. Because of the fragmentation of biology and the virtual abandonment of botany, the science of life has become the premise and pretext for the production of data and the transformation of bacteria into microscopic factories. Chargaff concludes, "In the tower of forlornness which the House of Science has become in my time, the inhabitants all speak the same language but do not understand each other."

Given the fact that the Central Dogma and its attendant assumptions and technical projects carry the highest aspirations of mechanistic, dualistic science, much more is at stake than a theory of heredity and epigenesis. One could say that a basic Western mission, the domestication of nature through the repair of Babel, is involved. For behind much of the scientific talk about the world as a collection of machines constructed by "selfish genes" is a deeply ingrained doubt, perhaps even a dread or fear, of a world that human beings have dedicated their long history either to modifying or forgetting.

Ilya Prigogine and Isabelle Stengers remind us in *Order Out of Chaos* (1983) that the mechanistic mode of life conceals a fundamental attitude toward the world:

> The words we still use today—machine, mechanical, engineer—have a similar meaning. They do not refer to rational knowledge but to cunning and expediency. The idea was not to learn about natural processes in order to utilize them more effectively, but to deceive nature, to "machinate" against it—that is to work wonders and create effects extraneous to the "natural order" of things.[19]

One of the classical formulations of the machine model was made by Jacques Loeb in *The Mechanistic Conception of Life* (1912). For Loeb, the mechanistic model was preferable to what he considered the metaphysical prejudices of those who spoke of a transcendent "harmony," or *Zielstrebigkeit*, which is necessary for all the elements of an organism to live. To speak of "wholeness" or "harmony" or "purposiveness" is, for Loeb, a "play on words . . . only an unclear expression for the fact that a species is only able to live . . . if it is provided with the *automatic mechanism* for self-preservation and reproduction" [my emphasis].[20] So powerful was the force of industrial culture that Loeb could dismiss "harmony" as a "metaphysical" term and employ "automatic mechanism" without the slightest sense that his own phrasing was no less a play on words. Ubiquitous as machines and automata had become by the twentieth century, they could serve as "natural" instances of transcendental modeling. Thus Monod urges us to recognize that "the cell is indeed a *machine*," presumably because by analyzing it according to such a model certain communal data can be reached, and certain wonders and "effects" achieved. Nature will be seduced into revealing her "secrets" and performing tricks. For Dawkins, the living world is nothing but DNA and the mechanical ruses it has invented for its survival. Monod, like Dawkins, sees the world as essentially "artificial," a representation, not of consciousness or mind, but of what appears to be its most elemental components. Seen in this light, molecular biology, as it has been popularized by Dawkins and others, represents an attempt to scientifically naturalize certain features of contemporary culture.

Monod's existentialist and Dawkins's free-market visions of nature may appear to be the stoic and brave acceptance of an indifferent and alien world. But they may simply be the most recent superstitions separating us from the world. For what the project of a nature revised and redeemed by technology promises (where perpetual health and even immortality are the products of modified viruses, bacteria, plants, animals, and human beings) is a mechanical and theatrical simulation of life—when the scientific Word will have finally become (a kind of) flesh.

Rupert Sheldrake of Cambridge University turned his back on this style of biology to study life outside the laboratory. He left England for India and worked at the Research Institute in Hyderabad, concentrating on the physiology of tropical legume plants. Following his return to England he published *A New Science of Life* (1981) which challenged the basic tenets of the Central Dogma. Sheldrake wrote that the power of DNA as an exemplary principle has been vastly exaggerated. The assumption that DNA and the respective genes which it composes guide the formation of the embryo and the growth of the body, the functioning of the body and even the mind, as well as carrying the particular characteristic of the parents is, he argues, unwarranted. The dogma was accepted credulously by the scientific and popular press because it confirmed the basic presupposition that life, like a machine, was the manifestation of an internal blueprint.[21]

The scientific press in Britain was outraged. *Nature* called the book "the best canditate for burning there has been for many years."[22] For by turning against the dominant model of nature as machine and trying to understand it as organic and natural, alien to the order of the machine, Sheldrake had offered a heretical explanation and opened the door to a host of supposedly metaphysical theories associated with animism, vitalism, and mysticism. But as Sheldrake argues, projection is hardly the question: it is a matter of which projection is acceptable to a mechanistic society and which is seen as fanciful and bizarre. "Ironically, the mechanistic approach itself seems to be *more* anthropomorphic than the animistic. It projects one particular kind of human activity, the construction and use of machines, onto the whole of nature. The mechanistic theory derives its plausibility precisely from the fact that machines *do* have purposive designs whose source is in living minds."

Sheldrake does not, however, simply object to this model on aesthetic or cultural grounds. He claims that DNA, even according to the mechanistic presumptions of its champions, is in itself not sufficient to explain the many tasks assigned to it. As Weismann insisted long before DNA was discovered, the germ plasm found in each cell would have to be different from cells in other parts of the body. But the identical strands of DNA are found in every cell of the body and produce identical proteins. And yet out of these proteins quite different forms arise: cells in the brain, leg, and foot develop from the same DNA program. Even dogmatists have come to recognize that the DNA molecule is not a complete and integral message that is simply transcribed by messenger RNA which in turn directs the formation of proteins, and so the form of the living body. And research has shown, as Sheldrake writes in his *The Pres-*

*ence of the Past* (1988), that "the total amount of DNA that is inherited seems to bear very little relationship to the complexity of the organism . . . the cells of lily plants contain thirty times more DNA than human cells." Moreover, the differences between the DNA in certain species of fruitflies are much greater than the differences between the genetic makeup of chimpanzees and human beings. Defenders of the Central Dogma could preserve their thesis by claiming that each cell only employs the information appropriate to it. In doing so, however, they would be creating the need for another source of guidance or information in the cell: a selector which would direct editing and transcription of the DNA. This would be the mysterious agency to which the passive voice piously defers.

Sheldrake advances his critique of the Central Dogma as a preface to one of the most audacious scientific hypotheses in modern times. Drawing on the antimechanistic critiques of Samuel Butler, Henri Bergson, and others, he proposes that the development of organic form is not ultimately governed from within by genetic information, but from without via what he calls "morphic resonance" and "formative causation." In essence, Sheldrake claims that organic form is an effect of all the previous organisms that have existed and that continue to direct the formation of living forms. A eucalyptus, a leopard, a human being are formed and shaped by resonances from their ancestors: each is an effect of memory. Far from the superstitious and occult properties which such a proposition suggests, Sheldrake's "resonance" is derived from C. H. Waddington's postulation of "individuation fields" and René Thom's translation of these fields into mathematical topologies. From a more comprehensive perspective, however, Sheldrake is drawing on the ancient tradition of "the great memory," postulated by Plato, Samuel Butler, and Yeats and joining it with modern organistic, holistic, and cybernetic thinking associated with Whitehead, Ludwig von Bertalannfy, and Gregory Bateson.

Organic form is guided, Sheldrake proposes, by the formal and behavioral influence of "past organisms of the same species through direct connections across space and time." DNA may "tune" these fields in the manner that a television receiver accepts and illustrates an electronic message. In this manner only can DNA be said to guide the production of protein and the growth of the body. Parental traits are not contained by genetic material, rather the genetic material receives and implements this resonance in a particular way. All living forms are enfolded within the memory of nature and within a past which is also present. In place of the information model of DNA, Sheldrake has substituted a much finer, but no less material medium, comparable to electromagnetic fields. The condescension or contempt of his critics notwithstanding, the idea of "formative fields' is no less occult than the orthodox view that a living form is the elaboration of the living "language" in a single molecule.

As evidence for the ways in which influence can be discovered even in the literature of modern science, Sheldrake cites experiments conducted by William McDougal at Harvard University in 1920 in which rats taught certain tasks seemed to pass on these acquired skills to their progeny. McDougal interpreted the results with reference to Lamarck's much-maligned belief in the inheritance of acquired characteristics. Subsequent tests on McDougall's findings by F. A. E. Crew at Edinburgh not only failed to refute the unacceptable findings, they exacerbated the anomaly: Crewe's rats learned even faster. Adding these data to anecdotal reports by animal trainers and breeders claiming that new generations of animals learned certain tasks more quickly than their ancestors, Sheldrake supposes that morphic resonance may be an explanation. The same kind of influence could be a solution to the question of why certain crystals formed for the first time in a laboratory seem to quicken the rate at which other crystals, separated by vast distances, form the same structure. A certain cumulative effect seems to become manifest within a species once its initial difficulty is overcome. It is this same principle, Sheldrake suggests, which guides the development of the embryo and the growth of the body.[23]

Thus the neo-Darwinist orthodoxy engages in a minute analysis of genetic structure, assuming implicitly that there is a kind of passive agency which sorts through and reads the language of DNA, while Sheldrake—with only circumstantial evidence—has named this agency. In both cases, nature has not spoken directly, as Heraclitus warned, but through signs. Monod reads, as it were, the determinate particle of our natural fate, just as Sheldrake sees an ongoing wave communicating between epochs and individuality and consciousness. And of course all of our cultural values persuade us that Monod and his colleagues are scientists and so are more or less right, and that Sheldrake is indulging his imagination, reviving old myths, and is most probably wrong.

And yet this mythological complexion scarcely distinguishes Sheldrake's hypothesis from Monod's existentialism. As long as geneticists ignore their implicit reliance upon an unspoken and unnameable agency, operating in the mysterious realm of the passive voice, which reads, targets, deletes, and edits organic "messages," they may as well admit that they need Sheldrake's morphic resonance, Samuel Butler's unconscious memory, or what Yeats once referred to as the "memory of nature." Still, one must respect their stoic resort to this least mythologized of metaphysical principles and to their search for refuge in the subterfuges of syntax, taking for comfort Heraclitus's axiom that nature loves to hide.

# 7

## Proust's Brain

Memory has thus three different aspects: memory when it remembers things, imagination when it alters or imitates them, and invention when it gives them a new turn or puts them into proper arrangement and relationship. For these reasons the theological poets called Memory the mother of the Muses.

—Vico, *The New Science*

Julian the Apostate, the Roman Emperor who returned the gods to the temples of the Mediterranean for a time, used to refer to the Christian churches as "charnel houses." He was referring not only to the obsessive topic of Christian art, the corpse of Christ, but also to the custom of placing the altarstone of every new church above the relic of a saint or martyr. The metacarpal or femur of a martyr, resting beneath the church built in his name, joined stone, mortar, and marble to the metaphysical seat of grace, which is God. In this way, the site where a priest's words are bound with the will of God is consecrated because, in part, it conceals a knucklebone or a thighbone.

Such was the model for the museums, archives, and crypts which were constructed during the Romantic Age and after to conserve, examine, and sometimes display the organs of great artists. The heart of Chopin was deposited at the Church of the Holy Cross in Warsaw; the brain of Whitman was entrusted to the American Anthropometric Association for measurement and description (where it was destroyed when a laboratory workman dropped it on the floor). Both the followers of Christ and the aesthetic faithful supposed that grace and genius were

115

matters related to bones and organs, that culture and form-
aldehyde equally preserved the legacy of extraordinary people.
By preserving such useless remains, it was thought that one
could stay in touch with more than the spiritual and artistic
legacies of saints and artists: it was as if they could be made
to witness their own apotheosis.

The corpus of an artist thus included not only the poems
he had written, the letters his correspondents had kept, and
various personal items (a guitar, an umbrella, a waistcoat), it
could include an organ emblematic of his genius. The heart of
Chopin testifies to the passion of the Preludes, the brain of
Whitman substantiates his identity with the cosmos. Well into
the twentieth century, at his own request, respectable insti-
tutions competed for Einstein's brain, as if the organ itself contained some clues to the origin of the theory of relativity. It
was in this tradition that the surgeon who operated on Italo
Calvino after his fatal cerebral hemorrhage observed that he
had never seen a brain of such "delicacy and complexity."[1]

Despite their different intellectual and spiritual assumptions,
the Church and Science acted upon an ancient, magical belief
that possessing a part could give one control over or knowledge
of the whole. Sir James Frazer called such thinking and practices "contagious magic," because both presume that things
which have once been in contact always remain somehow related or aligned.[2] If I possess one of your hairs, I may be able
to give you a headache; if I possess a saint's fingerbone, I may
have access to his grace; and if I have Chopin's heart or Whitman's brain, I may be in "touch" with their genius. This is the
fetishistic logic shared by primitives, Christians, aesthetes, and
scientists.

Of course, scientists argue that their interests in the brains
of exceptional people are not metaphysical but firmly based in
the observation of physical detail. Perhaps, after all, there was
something particular about the brain of Einstein that made him
more likely to understand that time was a fiction relative to a
particular planet moving at a steady velocity without reference
to other planets and velocities. Perhaps the brain of Walt Whitman could give scientists some preliminary idea of a corre-

spondence between qualities such as originality, cosmic consciousness, literary genius, and the size and features of the brain. In the same spirit, Calvino's surgeon may have assumed that there was a correspondence between the delicacy and complexity of the writer's brain and the same qualities in his writing. The surgeon must have felt the attraction of finding a symmetry between physical and spiritual facts. Such thinking supposes that there is a relationship between the organ which "thinks" and the texts which preserve those thoughts, but which only hands can write. Still, one cannot imagine an archive preserving the hand which wrote the complex and delicate lines of *Invisible Cities*: it would be too trivial a thing. But one wonders why.

Perhaps it is because many of the physical facts prized by modern culture are more like emblems of our values rather than simply evidence for their validity. Some facts are more significant than others, and these facts become emblems, symbols, and fetishes justified by virtue of their "factual" nature. We know that a brain is an organ weighing roughly three pounds and that it resembles the pale fruit of a large nut. It is certainly not the same as the mind, but it seems the best evidence we have for thinking that it is more than an abstraction for a reciprocal relationship between parts and wholes of the universe. The brain has consequently supplanted the mind and the soul as the most significant emblem of our own identity, the organic fact which seems to come closest to containing the irreducible evidence of our inmost nature. In fact, two of the more potent of contemporary emblems, the brain and the computer, are called into service to define one another. It is often not entirely clear which lends the greater prestige to the other.

According to Plato, our minds have only dim memories of the transcendental realm from which they derive the Ideas of Truth, Beauty, Justice, and Love. Our minds require an education, a drawing outward that is primarily an act of remembrance. By dialectic, an ignorant slave boy could be made to remember geometry, not to learn it.

For these reason, Plato was dead set against representations without an essential purpose: painting, writing, and acting were permissible only if they illustrated or facilitated the remembrance of the Ideas. In the *Phaedrus*, Socrates tells the tale of how the Egyptian god Thoth proudly brought his latest invention, writing, to the Pharaoh and was surprised to find condemnation when he had expected praise. According to the Pharaoh, writing would not facilitate "memory," but "recollection," an entirely different faculty. Trusting outward marks, the student would lose his own powers of memory and come to trust a simulation of wisdom, poetry, and analysis. Instead of fostering remembrance, the Pharaoh told Thoth, he would foster amnesia, for people would learn only the semblances of truth and not truth itself. Plato and the Pharaoh of the fable both condemn writing as the first violent dislocation of humanity from itself. The invention of writing, as well as all subsequent technologies of representation and communication, mark man's fall into simulated existence, and forever after he will seek to become an adequate version of what he sees in images. Writing, phonography, cinema, radio, and television all give an apparent "reality" by copying and re-presenting our ordinary sense perceptions. By presenting the symptoms of reality, these simulations are accepted as real. By adapting ourselves to them, we become the shadows of shadows, an even more pitiable condition than the shades of Achilles and Agamemnon who exist as memories of their eventful lives. People become images of other images, the shades of other shades: this is Plato's prescient condemnation of postmodern existence.

The graphic culture inspired by these inventions has made "natural" the idea that the brain preserves memory in the fashion of a writing tablet, a phonographic disc, a magnetic tape, a photographic record, or a highly developed computer. As fanciful or misleading as these metaphors are, one assumption outweighs them all in significance: our "selves," our "personalities," our "subjectivity" is but the image, projection, or simulation of the brain. Whatever the model, the assumption has been that the brain must preserve its knowledge of the past as a book preserves words: intellectual, emotional, and sensuous details are like so much neural script which becomes "activated" or "present" through an act of attention we have difficulty imagining, much less explaining. According to such thinking, then, memories belong to us, the way our eyes, our ears, and our tongues do. At the same time, it would be difficult to deny that we belong to our memories, habits, and prejudices.

In order to see how the brain is, however, a metaphorical explanation and substantiation of our supposedly unique identity as human beings, we might begin with something much simpler than considering the nature or meaning of remembering, thinking, or feeling. Simply consider the actions involved in the apparently passive act of "looking at" a tree—a laurel, for example.

Start by recalling that "seeing" is a particular faculty of our own. The tree does not see; it inhabits a world of heat and cold, qualities which we can identify with light and darkness, proximity and distance from the sun. For the laurel, wet and cold seasons are followed by dry and hot seasons, in an endless cycle. The tree "sees" only by eating the light which our eyes receive, focus, and pass on to our brains. The tree does not need to see; it requires only that the light strikes its leaves and initiates the chemical process called photosynthesis.

Like the tree, the eye cannot see. It is simply a ball containing a lense, aqueous humor, a retina, and the optic nerve which carries a "message" to the brain. Although it cannot see, the eye can receive, focus, and invert reflections of the lit world onto the retina. There the image is coded as an electrical impulse and is introduced into the neural system. We can follow the light in our mind's eye through the pupil, the humor, the retina, the optic nerve, and into the visual cortex of the brain. But we can never, never imagine, intuit, or see the moment or the place or the circumstances when electricity becomes sight. To do so would require that we posit some other seer of the seen, and so on in an infinite regress of seers and seens or scenes.

We can see instead that a series of transformations link the sun, the tree, the atmosphere, the eyes, the brain, and a man or a woman to the world. It is impossible to say that we see "with" our brain, although it is clear that we cannot see without it. The brain may simulate an image which "it" sees, but is no longer looking "at" anything other than itself. Thus the blind tree is dematerialized by the light and reimagined as a brain would imagine it. If we want to know what happens "inside" our brain, we have only to look at the tree. If we want to see the tree, we have to allow our brains to simulate it for us. We may imagine, then, that we look out at the world, but it would be equally true to say that the world looks into us— in order to be seen.

We can see this circular process in the myth of Apollo and Daphne.³ The young god, associated with both the sun and music, has fallen in love with this beautiful nymph. He pursues her at the speed of light, so to speak, but she manages to elude him because she has called on her father to preserve her virginity. The river-god Peneus spares the young god's prey, just as his hands are burning her thighs. In those fleeting moments she is metamorphosed into a laurel tree: her feet creep into the soil, her breasts and slender waist knot into bark, her straining arms and head yearn recklessly for the sky, her hair flutters like leaves in the light.

This is a photosynthesis by which the tree lives on the praise of her suitor and the suitor lives on the elusiveness of his desire. Ernst Cassirer notes the persistence of this myth within the Greek word for light (*phos*) folded into "Phoebus Apollo," the god whose "light" is in eternal pursuit of the laurel leaf.⁴

In this typically Western parable of perception and desire, the suitor is tragically denied the object of his passion. The logic of Ovid's poem is simple: desire thrives on loss, but out of this loss, the world becomes an image of human desire. Ovid's Mediterranean scenes are filled with flowers, trees, birds, and geologic formations which record the thwarted passions of human beings who sought to join themselves with their desires. To look at these scenes through Ovid and the literature which he inspired is to recognize our own situation. Like an Ovidian lover, we want to seize and possess a certain scene in a certain cast of light, while knowing the futility of our desire. What we are implicitly recognizing is not the impermanence of the light but our own insubstantiality: we see ourselves fading like light from the scene.

In the *Kena Upanishad*, a disciple asks his guru, "At whose behest does the mind think? Who bids the body live? Who makes the tongue speak? Who is that effulgent Being that directs the eye to form and color and ear to sound?"[5] In other words, who is it that sees what the "brain" re-presents, hears what the "brain" repeats, smells what the "brain" relays? It is a difficult question to answer because it forces us to realize, if we are to answer it forthrightly, that "we" cannot be the answer which is sought—if by the "self" we mean an intrinsic and isolated entity inside our bodies looking out at the world.

The guru answers: "Brahman (the World-Self) is the ear of the ear, mind of the mind, speech of speech. He is also breath of the breath, and eye of the eye. Having given up the false identification of the Self with the senses and the mind, and knowing the Self to be Brahman, the wise, on departing this life, become immortal." He becomes immortal, meaning he renounces and realizes the partiality of his own sense of identity. When the self becomes the Self, it is evident that there could be no seer of the seen, no hearer of the heard, no smeller of the smelt, no thinker of the thought, unless the two are indeed One. And if we have difficulty imagining the final seer of what is seen, perhaps that is because "he" is not necessary, not real, and simply an inference required by our dualistic approach to the world.

The brain appears then to be the best evidence for the assumption that "there is," or that "we have" an ego. But research into the brain reveals that such requirements of common sense are not easily satisfied. For the brain to serve as an "origin" for thoughts, emotions, and finally the self, it would have to be a single, integrated entity, with no parts inessential to these functions and principles. Anatomy, however, describes various parts of the brain without indicating its center, the point from which and toward which knowledge and will move—the brain of the brain. Surprisingly adaptable, the brain can manage to sustain its activities after massive and apparently fatal injuries.

Throughout the 1920s and 1930s the psychologist Karl Lashley attempted to locate memory traces by a process of elimination.[6] Destroying a portion of a rat's brain and then testing its abilities to recall and repeat certain patterns of behavior, he hoped to determine a correspondence between brain tissue and memory. In other words, he tried to establish the point of contact between the physical realm of the brain and the metaphysical realm of the mind. But despite having destroyed as much as eighty percent of the brain, he could not produce any appreciable failure of "memory." The memory traces or "engrams" thus could not be pinpointed. Since there was obviously no point-for-point relationship between the brain and "its" memories, he finally postulated that memories were distributed throughout the brain. In other words, if the brain contained memories at all, they could not be sensibly modeled on writing in the ordinary sense.

It might be profitable to consider memories from the point of view of the world which is itself remembered. If the *Kena Upanishad* is right in denying the mind of the mind, and the seer of the seen, perhaps we could consider memories in terms of what is remembered instead of how it is remembered and in what form it is preserved. But unless we credit the occult notion of something like an Akashic Record, which preserves everything that has ever taken place, we must conclude that our memories do not reside in any particular place. Perhaps they do not need to be re-presented to be re-membered. If we consider our own experiences, we might recognize the degree to which "our own" memories are distributed across the face of the world. If we stay in Los Angeles and try to remember the sights and smells of Pittsburgh, we will have only a limited success. But if we fly to Pittsburgh and walk the streets, much more than the immediate sensory stimulus will be recovered. More and more of "our" memories will come back, as if memories themselves have memories, and those memories have memories as well, and so on indefinitely. Without the brain, we imagine, our memories might recede into the texture of reality: cities, houses, trees, smells, tastes, and shades of light would absorb our past, and with it our innermost "self." The brain alone would appear to substantiate what the *Upanishads* consider the pernicious illusion of a separate ego. Neurological investigations into the preservation of memory thus also call into question the possibility of intellectually maintaining the idea of a "self."

Even writing, which has inspired most thinking about memory formation, may not really preserve memories in any coherent sense. As much as Marcel Proust put into his novels, no one is in a position to determine in what sense they constitute an imaginative transformation of his memories. If memory, as Marcel (the putative narrator and hero of the novels) often supposes, is an imaginative faculty, then it is quite possible that fiction is the most responsible way to preserve it, just as writing one's "memoirs" would be the most misleading. In either case, the reader can scarcely be expected to keep his mind on "what he is reading," since he cannot be certain what the substance of written words are. Instead, he becomes increasingly absorbed in a narrative concerning characters, such as Monsieur Swann and his daughter Gilberte, who are based on characters of Proust's own acquaintance. But these fictional characters not only reflect and distort characters Proust knew, they also describe characters that we know. Reading of Marcel's mother recalls our own mother; Gilberte recalls a childhood infatuation (since "forgotten"); M. Swann recalls a mysterious and worldly friend of the family. Proust recalls and recreates characters, but we read their details as reflections of our own memories. Things which we have forgotten (the sound of a bell, the muffled conversation of adults heard from one's darkened room) come to light because, in effect, Proust has remembered them for us.

When the middle-aged Marcel dips his madeleine in tea and tastes it, he opens an apparently direct passage to his childhood in Combray. Out of this passage comes *A la recherche du temps perdu* and out of Proust's work has come a series of parallel universes for his many committed readers in French and other languages. Not that the whole of this work of some one and a quarter million words is a directly sensual influx of involuntary memory. But it is by virtue of this experience that Marcel discovers his vocation, which is to demonstrate that, as Kant argued, Time and Space are but artificial, porous constructions of consciousness:

And as in the game wherein the Japanese amuse themselves by filling a porcelain bowl with water and steeping in it little pieces of paper which until then are without character or form, but, the moment they become wet, stretch and twist and take on colour and distinctive shape, so in that moment all the flowers in our garden and in M. Swann's park, and the water-lilies of the Vivonne and the good folk of the village and their little dwellings and the parish church and the whole of Combray and its surroundings, taking shape and solidity, sprang into being, town and gardens alike, from my cup of tea.[7]

Involuntary memory and the Japanese game both work by unfolding (or ex-plaining) the "contents" of a folded or compressed element. As the madeleine is dipped in tea, so is the paper immersed in water: Marcel is similarly dipped into a sensory fluid by which he expands and unfolds the whole of his memories. The image of folding and unfolding unfolds other images of the same, and each would appear to unfold others. In a similar way the brain is supposed to infold memories within its convoluted hemispheres, and preserve them until such time as they are properly stimulated. The neurosurgeon Wilder Penfield discovered that, by touching certain points of the exposed brain of a waking patient, he could evoke specific memories which were then experienced with complete sensual detail. A young woman reported during this procedure, once a particular electrode had fired, "Yes, I heard voices down along the river somewhere—a man's voice and a woman's voice calling. . . . I think I saw the river."[8] Memory is the result, then, of the meeting of elements long separated: tea and madeleine, paper and water, specific neurons and electricity. Their meeting unfolds a vivid representation of what was always immanent, but inaccessible.

Penfield's ability to recreate memories would appear to refute Lashley's claim that memories cannot be strictly associated with a single point in the cerebral cortex. Although he rightly took credit for stimulating one vivid scene by stimulating one precise point on the brain, Penfield and his colleague Herbert Jasper made no such claims:

It is obvious that there is, beneath the electrode, a recording mechanism, for memories of events. But the mechanism seems to have recorded much more than the simple event. When activated, it may produce the emotions which attended the original experience. . . . It seems obvious that such duplicating recording patterns can only be performed in the cerebral cortex after there has been complete co-ordination or integration of all the nerve impulses that passed through both hemispheres—that is to say, all the nerve impulses that are associated with or result from the experience. It seems to be the integrated whole that is recorded.[9]

In other words, when we speak of preserving "one" memory, much more, necessarily, is involved. One could say that the whole of one's "emotional" life is encoded in every "memory," because without such a coding such emotions could not become accessible. Penfield's physiology confirms at the physical level Freud's notion that all human actions, and the emotions which are indissociable from them, rise out of an unconscious nexus of associations.

Our ordinary notion of specific memories is not supported by such a neurological description. Trying to locate a single memory would be like trying to take the stain out of a sweater by pulling at the offending threads: the point dissolves into a tangle. And if the single memory is an illusory entity, woven as it is within, and implying as it does, the whole of one's past (which is to say everything in one's mind), then the same might be said of the brain as well. For the brain is no less woven into the circuitry of nerves, the circulation of the blood, and the unceasing stimulus of the world. Sir Charles Sherrington compared the human brain to "an enchanted loom where millions of flashing shuttles weave a dissolving pattern, always a meaningful pattern, though never an abiding one. . . . It is as if the Milky Way entered upon some cosmic dance."[10]

Proust's novels dramatize these principles by showing how the sum of a man's life can be extrapolated from the taste of tea and madeleine, even when the past would appear completely lost to memory and interest:

When from a long-distant past nothing subsists, after the people are dead, after the things are broken and scattered, taste and smell alone, more fragile but more enduring, more unsubstan-

> tial, more persistent, more faithful, remain poised a long time,
> like souls, remembering, waiting, hoping, amid the ruins of all
> the rest; and bear unflinchingly, in the tiny and almost im-
> palpable drop of their essence, the vast structure of recollec-
> tion.[11]

Taste and smell, Proust claims, combine fragility and perma-
nence, just as souls, said to be immaterial and eternal, do. But
what are taste and smell if not the ghosts of "our" experiences
which haunt the world, not us. We require the taste and the
smell of tea, a certain pastry, a specific street, or a forgotten
toy to "recollect" ourselves. This means, then, to gather up,
to recollect elements of ourselves that have been scattered
across the world, and have taken residence in more or less
insensate things. It was this recognition that led ancient peoples to speak of metamorphoses, the genius of a place (*genius
loci*), and the transmigration of souls.

Proust follows in this tradition by expressing an unrequited
desire for the world that we find in Ovid's tale of Apollo and
Daphne. After Marcel discovers Albertine in the "little band"
of girl bicyclists at the seaside, he uses a metaphor that recalls
an Ovidian metamorphosis:

> at the far end of the esplanade, along which they projected a
> striking patch of color, I saw five or six young girls as different
> in appearance and manner from all the people one was accus-
> tomed to see at Balbec as would have been a flock of gulls
> arriving from God knows where and performing with measured
> tread upon the sands—the dawdlers flapping wings to catch up
> with the rest—a parade the purpose of which seems as obscure
> to the human bathers whom they do not appear to see as it is
> clearly determined in their own birdish minds.[12]

In subsequent passages, the girls are compared to "statues exposed to the sunlight on a Grecian shore" as well as bands of,
respectively, "Hellenic virgins," "Dianas," and "nymphs."
Marcel can see things which matter to him only through a
series of metaphoric and mythological elaborations. The effect
is to make the girls, and Albertine in particular, into the focus
of his extensive desire, the center of gravity toward which
mythology, art, and history are drawn. These three spheres of

aesthetic experience coincide in Marcel's perception of the little band, because they can be read as if they were features of the Mediterranean seascapes which Ovid describes.

In *The Metamorphoses* we read how Ino and the Theban women when fleeing from the mad Athamas cast themselves into the sea. Seeing this, Venus beseeches Neptune to preserve them and her wish is granted: some become sea birds and others become stony features in the Mediterranean shoreline. It is this myth and this seascape that Marcel sees in the girl cyclists playing on the seacoast of Normandy. Experience itself becomes a form of memory.

On the other hand, memory can be the most direct kind of experience. During another vacation at Balbec, Marcel is suddenly overtaken by the apparent presence of his recently deceased grandmother. While bending down to take off his boots, he is "filled with an unknown, a divine presence" and is "shaken with sobs." Until this moment, Marcel explains, he had yet to experience the reality of her death because he had yet to remember her being alive and completely well. Out of this paradoxical experience, Marcel derives certain conclusions concerning the nature and "location" of memory:

> At any given moment, our total soul has only a more or less fictitious value, in spite of the rich inventory of its assets, for now some, now others are unrealisable, whether they are real riches or those of the imagination. . . . For with the perturbations of memory are linked the intermittencies of the heart. It is, no doubt, the existence of our body, which we may compare to a vase enclosing our spiritual nature, that induces us to suppose that all our inner wealth, our past joys, all our sorrows, are perpetually in our possession. Perhaps it is equally inexact to suppose that they escape or return. In any case if they remain within us, for most of the time it is in an unknown region where they are of no use to us, and where even the most ordinary are crowded out by memories of a different kind, which preclude any simultaneous occurrence of them in our consciousness.[13]

Our bodies give us a fictitious sense of spiritual integrity and isolation, in other words. From our bodies we derive the idea that our selves, our memories, our minds must be distinct and isolated. But this image of the body as a distinct and self-contained form is an illusory one. Since the body can see for miles, imagine and calculate the future, re-experience the past, breathe air, thrive on plants and animals, how could one suppose that it is distinct and isolated from all of these sources of its life. In this same way, the image of the soul, the self, and the self-possessed memory is an illusory one, modeled on the figure of this isolated body.

Frustrated by the scientific orthodoxy which claimed that all mental and emotional phenomena must be explained by the fundamental, physical composition of the body and brain, a number of established scientists in the 1970s began to rethink the basically reductive, Newtonian premises of neuroscience. Roger Sperry of the California Institute of Technology, reviewing these developments in the August, 1988, issue of *American Psychologist*, writes, "over the last 15 years, changes in the foundational concepts of psychology instituted by the new cognitive or mentalist paradigm have radically reformed scientific descriptions of human nature and the conscious self. The resultant views today are less atomistic, less mechanistic, and more mentalistic, contextual, subjectivist, and humanistic." The fundamental breakthrough registered by this trend in neuroscience is the recognition that mental activities cannot be understood strictly from the microstructure of the brain: "The supervenient control exerted by the higher over lower level properties of a system, referred to also as 'macro', 'molar', or 'emergent' determinism, operates concurrently with the 'micro' control from below upward. Mental states, as emergent properties of brain activity, thus exert downward control over their constituent neuronal events." Sperry concludes that this "new outlook puts subjective mental forces near the top of the brain's causal control hierarchy and gives them primacy in determining what a person is and does."[14]

Extending the scope of this critique of purely "physical" determinism, Karl Pribram, a neuropsychologist at Stanford University, and David Bohm, a physicist at London University, have proposed a theory that would account for the relationship between the supposedly discrete realms of bodies and minds, matter and consciousness, the world and memory. According to Pribram and Bohm, both the brain and the universe might well be organized according to the same logic of the folding and unfolding of wholes and particulars. Just as a holographic, three-dimensional image is constructed in such a way that each of its parts contains an image of the whole, so the brain could be said to electrically infold the whole within each of its parts. Bohm has postulated that the universe is itself organized according to the same principle: the explicit or unfolded universe is structured by an "implicate order," an infolded unity, which means that each "part" of the universe "contains" the whole. The brain and the universe may be structured according to the same holographic logic. Pribram explains the consequences of such thinking this way:

> At the moment this order appears so indistinguishable from the mental operations by which we operate on that universe that we must conclude either that our science is a huge mirage, a construct of the emergence of our convoluted brains, or that indeed, as proclaimed by all the great religous convictions, a unity characterizes this emergent [consciousness] and the basic order of the universe.[15]

Soon after she has become his captive, Marcel finds Albertine sleeping and discovers something of this implicit order:

> By shutting her eyes, by losing consciousness, Albertine had stripped off, one after another, the different human personalities with which she had deceived me ever since the day when I had first made her acquaintance. She was animated now only by the unconscious life of plants, of trees, a life more different from my own, more alien, and yet one that belonged more to me. . . . I had the impression of possessing her entirely which I never had when she was awake.[16]

There may be some wisdom after all in Marcel's infatuation with the banal Albertine, the girl cyclist in whom he sees the mythologies, the unthinkable future, and the somnolent powers of the natural world. Like those early Christians who preserved relics in hopes of substantiating spirit, or those romantic scientists who examined the brains of Byron, Whitman, and Einstein in order to see the organic basis of their genius, or these distinguished scientists who argue that the world is enfolded in each of its "parts," Marcel hopes that the particular body of Albertine is in fact everything she has come to represent for him. For this to be true, however, she must remain the unknown girl by the seashore, be found asleep, or be remembered after she has left him, and died. The art of memory in Proust's novels is not, then, simply a nostalgic recreation of the past, predicated upon the principle that we love only that which is distant or absent. Memory is shown to be the particular and inevitable infolding within the world of which we are both a conscious and material part. This infolding sometimes manifests itself as a distance from others, and even from ourselves. But this distance is the very condition of our relationship with the world, which often appears to be the bitterest alienation and isolation: a brain, a mind, alone in a material world of unthinking and unfeeling process. And we remain, strangely enough, an aspect of this unfeeling and unthinking process until we recognize that the self is not the mental aura of a single body and a single brain. This is what the loss and recovery of Time signifies in Proust and what he has to teach us.

# 8

# The Silence of Rivers

I remember a mark on a clay-colored building in Florence indicating how high the Arno had reached during the worst of the flooding in 1966. Despite the personal and hasty nature of the mark and the few simple words ("ecco, il diluvio, 1966"), there was an unmistakable bravado in the gesture. While the world sent money to preserve the paintings at the Uffizi, there was at least one Florentine who may have relished the fact that the red flood of the Arno had done its worst and he and his city had survived. The slashed mark and words attest to that fact, and so does the docile and silent movement of the river beneath the Ponte Vecchio. Both are memorials, but in different ways.

The river's every movement recollects every movement it has ever made: each nearly silent splash and jostled rush forward both recalls and foretells other movements. But a mark on a wall, even if it only deepens the muddy stain left by the river, is meant to escape from the circulation of time and enter a motionless and permanent space. And with it a single author, even if anonymous like this one, and a single year achieve a local insularity in the flow of time. The mark, with its words and numbers, recollects an exceptional moment, but the river recalls in silence, in a necessary oblivion.

A memory without a self may well appear to be the opposite of recollection, simply an anonymous process. But this appears only from the viewpoint of the self whose very existence depends upon a separation from the world and so considers natural the idea that memory is a discrete fragment rescued from the past. But if a memory is comprehensive and powerful enough to sweep away the solitary self, it can blend with oblivion.

The history of memory is a long one, and yet it seems to fall into three discrete chapters: oral recollection, writing, and electronic storage and video display. So powerful was the break between oral cultures and literate cultures that even now we consider that history begins only when it can be found written on a scroll or graven on a wall. And indeed in several centuries, when the globe will be knotted into a single circuitry carrying new myths, perhaps our own humanist age, stretching intermittently from Plato to Heidegger, will appear as quaint, obscure, and strangely unreal. It may well be seen as the epoch before "information," which flows with the speed, fluidity, and clarity of electricity, displaced the complexities of written "knowledge." The denizens of the future will probably look to us as we look back to the preliterate era: with a mixture of romantic infatuation, condescension, and skepticism. This is because the culture-bearing medium of recollection, whether it is the chanted word, the silent mark, or the humming electronic image, promotes an ineluctable loyalty, creating, transforming, or dissolving subjectivities and worlds.

The originative memory is organism itself, the persistence of organized patterns and cycles passing from stars to rivers to bodies. We tend to think of memory as the possession of an individual ego, but it is perhaps more accurate to see that the individual ego is remembered—or lives—because of the patterned forces of organic memory. The cardio-vascular system is autonomic (or self-ruling) only because of the millions of years of accumulated memory implicit in each breath and heartbeat. Cybernetic theorists recognize this fact, but they refer to an organism in this general sense as a feedback system. Such phrasing cannot conceal its mythological basis: a system is very like an abstracted river, the originative image of cyclicity. And our body, Novalis wrote, is a moulded river.[1]

Mythologies remember the organism by repeating its patterns in human terms, but mythological peoples are not interested in how uniform or consistent these narratives are. According to Lévi-Strauss, a myth, therefore, is the whole repertoire of retellings and modifications which a culture produces with respect to certain themes or topics.[2] There is both a certain piety and a certain disregard implicit in this: mythological peoples realize that they cannot—and do not want to—replace the extravagant and finally mysterious processes of nature with a single and totalized myth. Before all the painted walls, books of the dead, and ritual verse in ancient Egypt, there is the unwritten myth of Osiris. If one wants to see the original of this story, whose text we can find complete only in Plutarch, we have to turn to the Nile. It is on this river that Osiris's dismembered body floats until it arrives at the papyrus swamps of "Byblos."

The terminus of Byblos: this is the last stop of memory, when it becomes a text. The Book exercises all the ingenuity and ruses of writing, the entire repertoire of rhetorical devices, in order to somehow contain and reveal the process of the whole. Works like *A la recherche du temps perdu* are, from a mythological perspective, vain attempts to render the complexity and completeness of the world in a single form. But then the mythic cycle continues in our postmodern age, if perhaps in a minor mode, when interpretation becomes the heroic endeavor of those who see in such texts an instance of the ineffable, the inexhaustible, or the sacred.

All the arts of memory attempt to trick oblivion by making the past somehow present, whether through voice, writing, or magnetic disk. In doing this, the fundamental ground of oblivion itself is forgotten, and in its place people become satisfied with—indeed demand—simulated existence. For in a sense, the power of forgetfulness, the silence of rivers, is its ability to encompass the whole process, past, present, and future, in which all life and thought move. It is in this sense that religions the world over speak of God, Brahman, Yahweh, Allah, the Tao, as forgotten. And it is in this sense too that Christians, Jews, Muslims, Buddhists, and Hindus all speak of a fall from grace, wholeness, and spirit into time and history—and the labors of recollection. For if memory is a gift, forgetting is a kind of grace.

# Notes


## Introduction

1. Marcel Proust, *Remembrance of Things Past*, translated by C. K. Scott Moncrieff and Terence Kilmartin (New York: Vintage, 1981), vol. 2, 625.

2. J. H. Breasted, *The Dawn of Conscience* (New York: Scribners, 1950), 272–303.

## 1. Unconscious Cities

1. See the discussion of Baudelaire and Walter Benjamin in Susan Buck-Morss, *The Dialectics of Seeing: Walter Benjamin and the Arcades Project* (Cambridge: The MIT Press, 1989), 177–185.

2. Paul Valéry, "The Crisis of the Mind," in *An Anthology*, edited by James R. Lawler (Princeton: Princeton University Press, 1977), 97.

3. Ezra Pound, *Personae* (New York: New Directions, 1971).

4. Sigmund Freud, "A Disturbance of Memory on the Acropolis," translated by James Strachey, reprinted in *Character and Culture* (New York: Collier, 1963), 311–320.

5. Sigmund Freud, *The Future of an Illusion*, translated by W. D. Robson-Scott and James Strachey (New York: Doubleday, 1964), 38.

6. Sigmund Freud, *Civilization and its Discontents*, translated by James Strachey (New York: Norton, 1961), 17–18.

7. "A Note upon the 'Mystic Writing Pad'" in *General Psychological Theory* (New York: Collier, 1963), 207–212.

8. Charles Baudelaire, *Les Paradis artificiels* (Paris: Garnier-Flammarion, 1966), 145.

9. Sigmund Freud, *The Complete Psychological Works* (New York: Norton), edited by James Strachey, vol. 13, 177–178.

10. See C. G. Jung, *Memories, Dreams, Reflections*, translated by Richard and Clara Winston (New York: Vintage, 1965), 284–288, for Jung's account of his visit to Ravenna and his plans to visit Rome.

11. Sigmund Freud, *The Origins of Psychoanalysis: Letters to Wilhelm Fliess, Drafts, and Notes, 1887–1902*, translated by Eric Mosbacher and James Strachey (New York: Basic Books, 1954), 236, 269, 294.

12. Sigmund Freud, *The Interpretation of Dreams*, translated by James Strachey (New York: Avon, 1965), 229.

13. T. S. Eliot, *Collected Poems: 1909–1962* (New York: Harcourt, Brace, 1963). Subsequent quotations from Eliot are taken from this volume.

14. Jung, *Memories, Dreams, Reflections*, 287.

15. See *A Buddhist Bible*, edited by Dwight Goddard (Boston: Beacon Press, 1970), 280–282.

16. Walter Benjamin, "Paris: Capital of the Nineteenth Century," reprinted in *Reflections*, translated by Edmund Jephcott (New York: Harcourt, Brace, Jovanovitch, 1978), 146–162.

17. Ezra Pound, *Guide to Kulchur* (New York: New Directions, 1968), 57.

## 2. Dreaming of Egypt

1. Peter Tompkins, *The Secrets of the Great Pyramid* (New York: Harper and Row, 1971), 55.

2. Hilda Doolittle, *Collected Poems: 1912–1944* (New York: New Directions, 1983), 509.

3. Percy Bysshe Shelley, *Selected Poetry*, edited by Neville Rogers (London: Oxford, 1968), 340.

4. Unless otherwise noted all citations from Hegel are taken from G. W. F. Hegel, *The Philosophy of History*, translated by J. Sibree (New York: Dover, 1956), 198–215.

5. G. W. F. Hegel, *The Philosophy of Mind*, translated by William Wallace and A. V. Miller (Oxford: Clarendon Press, 1971), 213.

6. Jacques Derrida, *Margins of Philosophy*, translated by Alan Bass (Chicago: University of Chicago Press, 1982), 77.

7. Albertine Gaur, "The Story of Writing," British Library Exhibition Notes, 1984, 1–4.

8. Charles Baudelaire, *Les Paradis artificiels*, 35–36.

9. Sigmund Freud, *The Interpretation of Dreams*, 129–130, 154, 377, 522.

10. Sergei Eisenstein, "The Cinematographic Principle and the Ideogram," translated by Jay Leyda, in *Film Forum: Essays in Film Theory* (New York: Harcourt, Brace & World, 1949), 29, 32–34, 65.

11. René Clair, "Writing in Images," translated by Stanley Appelbaum, *Cinema Yesterday and Today* (New York: Dover, 1972), 69–70, 105.

12. Jacques Derrida, *Of Grammatology*, translated by Gayatri Chakravorty Spivak (Baltimore: Johns Hopkins University Press, 1976), 3, 20.

13. Sir E. A. Wallis Budge, *The Gods of the Egyptians: Studies in Egyptian Mythology* (New York: Dover, 1969; originally published 1904), vol. 1, 143.

14. Jacques Derrida, *Glas*, translated by John P. Leavey and Richard Rand (Lincoln: University of Nebraska Press, 1987), 256a.

15. Jacques Derrida, *Of Grammatology*, 80.

16. Michel Serres, *Hermes: Literature, Science, Philosophy*, edited by Josué Harari and David F. Bell (Baltimore: Johns Hopkins University Press, 1982), 87, 91.

17. G. W. F. Hegel, *The Philosophy of Fine Art*, translated by F. P. B. Osmaston (London: Bell, 1920), vol. 3, 52–53.

18. Herodotus, *The Histories*, translated by Aubrey de Selincourt (Harmondsworth: Penguin, 1954), 178.

19. Hegel, *The Philosophy of Fine Art*, vol. 3, 52–53.

20. Ahmed Fakhry, *The Pyramids* (Chicago: University of Chicago Press, 1961), 103, 124.

21. Peter Tompkins, *The Secrets of the Great Pyramid*, xiii, xiv.

22. Sigmund Freud, *Beyond the Pleasure Principle*, translated by James Strachey (New York: Norton, 1961), 32.

23. Nicolas Abraham and Maria Torok, *Cryptonomie: Le Verbier de l'homme aux loups* (Paris: Flammarion, 1976), 114–115.

24. Julian Jaynes, *The Origin of Consciousness in the Breakdown of the Bicameral Mind* (Boston: Houghton Mifflin, 1976), 188.

25. Sigmund Freud, *Three Essays on the Theory of Sexuality*, translated by James Strachey (New York: Basic Books, 1975), 41–42.

26. Derrida, *Margins of Philosophy*, 3–4.


## 3. INMOST INDIA

1. *The Works of Sir William Jones* (London, 1807), vol. 3, 1–2.

2. See *The Letters of Sir William Jones*, edited by Garland Cannon (Oxford: Clarendon Press, 1970), vol. 2, 683, 684, 740.

3. *The Works of Sir William Jones*, vol. 7, 89–90, 76.

4. *The Works of Sir William Jones*, vol. 3, 185–204.

5. See Friedrich Schlegel, *On the Language and Wisdom of the Indians* in *The Aesthetic and Miscellaneous Works of Frederick von Schlegel*, translated by E. J. Millington (London: Bohn, 1849), 429, 454–456, 472–473.

6. See Friedrich Schlegel, *The Philosophy of Life and Philosophy of Language*, translated by the Rev. A. J. W. Morrison, M.A. (London: Bohn, 1847), 407, 412.

7. Hegel, *The Philosophy of History*, 139–143.

8. Jung, *Memories, Dreams, Reflections*, 274–284.

9. See Peter Goodchild, *J. Robert Oppenheimer: Shatterer of Worlds* (New York: Fromm, 1985), 162.

10. *Bhagavad-Gita As It Is*, translated by A. C. Bhaktivedanta (The Bhaktivedanta Book Trust, 1983).

11. I refer to the eleven-hour performance of Peter Brook's and Jean-Claude Carrière's adaptation of the *Mahabharata* in Los Angeles, September, 1987.

12. *Srimad Bhagavatam Purana*, translated by A. C. Bhaktivedanta (The Bhaktivedanta Book Trust, 1972), vol. 1, 363–374.

13. James Joyce, *Finnegans Wake* (New York: Viking Press, 1939), 353.

14. Werner Heisenberg, *Physics and Beyond* (New York: Harper Torchbooks, 1972), 41.

15. Erwin Schrödinger, *My View of the World*, translated by Cecily Hastings (Cambridge: Cambridge University Press, 1964), 7.

16. Alfred North Whitehead, *Science and the Modern World* (New York: Macmillan, 1972), 50–55.

17. Schrödinger, *My View of the World*, 19.

18. Schrödinger, *Science, Theory, and Man* (New York: Dover, 1957), 190.

19. Schrödinger, *My View of the World*, 20–21, 28.

20. Benjamin Lee Whorf, *Language, Thought, and Reality* (Cambridge: The MIT Press, 1962), 269.

21. Asvaghosa, *The Awakening of Faith*, translated by D. T. Suzuki (London: Open Court, 1900), 104.

22. Jeremy Bernstein, *Science Observed* (New York: Basic Books, 1982), 339.

23. On Alexander in India see S. Radhakrishna, *History of Philosophy, Eastern and Western* (London: Allen and Unwin, 1952), vol. 1, 34.

24. Arrian, *The Campaigns of Alexander*, translated by Aubrey de Selincourt (Harmondsworth: Penguin, 1971), 349–352, 356–357.

25. R. F. Gould, *Collected Essays and Papers Relating to Freemasonry* (Belfast: Tait, 1913), 271.

26. Rudyard Kipling, "The Man Who Would be King," collected in *The Phantom Rickshaw* (vol. 5), 77, 80, *The Works of Rudyard Kipling* (New York: Scribner's, 1898).

27. "The Ballad of East and West," collected in *Verses* (vol. 11), 61, *The Works of Rudyard Kipling* (New York: Scribners, 1898).

## 4. The Word of Galaxy

1. James Joyce, *Ulysses* (New York: Vintage, 1986), 573–574.

2. Sir Charles Sherrington, *Man on His Nature* (New York: Doubleday, 1953), 184.

3. Charles F. Stevens, "The Neuron," *Scientific American*, vol. 241, no. 3 (September 1979), 55.

4. Cited by Hans Jonas, *The Gnostic Religion* (Boston: Beacon Press, 1963), 63.

5. Carl Jung, *Flying Saucers: A Modern Myth*, in volume 10, *The Collected Works of C. G. Jung*, edited by Sir Herbert Read (Princeton: Princeton University Press, 1970).

6. Francis Cornford, *Plato's Cosmology: The Timaeus of Plato* (London: Routledge & Kegan Paul, 1948), 142–146.

7. Giorgio de Santillana, *The Origins of Scientific Thought* (Chicago: University of Chicago Press, 1961), 56–57.

8. See *Tao Te Ching*, translated by Gia-Fu Feng and Jane English (New York: Vintage, 1989), chapter 11.

9. Immanuel Kant, *The Critique of Practical Judgment*, translated by Thomas Kingsmill Abbott (Chicago: William Benton, 1952), 360–361.

10. Immanuel Kant, "Universal Natural History," translated and edited by W. Hastie in *Kant's Cosmogony* (Glasgow: Maclehose, 1900), 30, 53.

11. Lewis White Beck, *A Commentary on Kant's Critique of Practical Reason* (Chicago: University of Chicago Press, 1960), 282.

12. Immanuel Kant, *The Critique of Judgment*, translated by James Creed Meredith (Chicago: William Benton, 1952), 504.

13. Sigmund Freud, *New Introductory Lectures*, translated by James Strachey (New York: Norton, 1966), 525, 538, 627.

14. Immanuel Kant, *Critique of Practical Judgment*, 361.

15. Stephen Hawking, *A Brief History of Time* (New York: Bantam, 1988), 124–126.

16. John Gribbin and Martin Rees, *Cosmic Coincidences: Dark Matter, Mankind, and Anthropic Cosmology* (New York: Bantam, 1989), 11.

## 5. The Metaphor of the Shell

1. See Wordsworth, *The Prelude: Growth of a Poet's Mind* (Oxford: Oxford University Press, 1970), Book 5, "On Books."

2. See Jane Worthington Smyser, "Wordsworth's Dream of Literature and Science," *Publications of the Modern Language Association*, 81 (March 1956), 269–275.

3. See Gregor Sebba, *The Dream of Descartes* (Carbondale: Southern Illinois University Press, 1987), 5–29, for this and subsequent references to Descartes's dreams.

4. *The Prelude*, Book 6, "Cambridge and the Alps."

5. Gaston Bachelard, *The Poetics of Space*, translated by Maria Jolas (Boston: Beacon Press, 1969), 113–114.

6. Paul Valéry, "Man and the Seashell" in *Paul Valéry: An Anthology*, 112, 118.

7. Le Corbusier, *The Modulor: A Harmonious Measure to the Human Scale* (Cambridge: The MIT Press, 1968).

8. George E. Duckworth, *Structural Patterns and Proportions in Vergil's Aeneid* (Ann Arbor: University of Michigan Press, 1962), 37–39, 61–63.

9. D'Arcy Wentworth Thompson, *Growth and Form* (Cambridge: Cambridge University Press, 1952), vol. 2, 750, 757, 849.

10. See Ilya Prigogine and Isabelle Stengers, *Order Out of Chaos*

(New York: Bantam, 1984) on the Belousov-Zhabotinsky reaction, 151–153.

11. Lucretius, *On the Nature of the Universe*, translated by R. E. Latham (Harmondsworth: Penguin, 1986), 66 [book 2].

12. Gregory Bateson, *Mind and Nature: A Necessary Unity* (New York: Bantam, 1980), 3–23.

13. Charles Darwin, *Voyage of the Beagle* (Harmondsworth: Penguin, 1989), 245.

14. James Lovelock, *Gaia: A New Look at Life on Earth* (Oxford: Oxford University Press, 1979), 10.

15. Erich Jantsch, *The Self-Organizing Universe: Scientific and Human Implications of the Emerging Paradigm of Evolution* (Oxford: Pergamon, 1980).

## 6. The Memory of Nature

1. Richard Dawkins, *The Selfish Gene* (New York: Oxford University Press, 1976), 3.

2. Leibniz, *New Essays on Human Understanding*, translated by Peter Remnant and Jonathan Bennet (Cambridge: Cambridge University Press, 1981), #337.

3. On Boehme, see Hans Aarsleff, *From Locke to Saussure: Essays on the Study of Language and Intellectual History* (Minneapolis: University of Minnesota Press, 1982), 56–69.

4. See Haig P. Papazian, *Modern Genetics* (New York: Norton, 1967), 28–31.

5. William Bateson, *Materials for the Study of Variations* (London: Macmillan, 1894).

6. August Weissman, *The Germ-Plasm: A Theory of Heredity*, translated by W. Newton Parker and Harriet Ronnfeldt (New York: Scribners, 1898), 32.

7. E. Margoliash, "Informational Macromolecules and Biological Evolution" in *The Heritage of Copernicus: Theories "Pleasing to the Mind,"* edited by Jerzy Neyman (Cambridge: The MIT Press, 1974), 188.

8. James D. Watson, *The Double Helix* (New York: Signet, 1969), 13–21, 28, 30.

9. Erwin Chargaff, "Building the Tower of Babble," *Nature* 248 (April 26, 1974), 776–779.

10. *The Double Helix*, 98.

11. Jacques Monod, *Chance and Necessity*, translated by Austryn Wainhouse (Glasgow: Collins, 1974), 96–97, 160.

12. Richard Dawkins, *The Selfish Gene*, 22.

13. Jean Baudrillard, *Simulations*, translated by Paul Foss, Paul Patton, and Philip Beitchman (New York: Semiotexte, 1983), 103–113.

14. Joan Artgetsinger Steitz, "Snurps," *Scientific American*, June 1988, 56–58.

15. Janet M. Shaw, Jean E. Feagin, Kenneth Stuart, and Larry Simpson, "Editing of Kinetoplastid Mitochondrial mRNAs by Uridine Addition and Deletion Generates Conserved Amino Acid Sequences and AUG Initiation Codons," *Cell*, vol. 53 (May 6, 1988), 401–411.

16. John Cairns, Julie Overbaugh, and Stephan Miller, "The Origins of Mutants," *Nature* 33 (September 8, 1988), 142–145.

17. Jacques Monod, *Chance and Necessity*, 36.

18. Richard Dawkins, *The Selfish Gene*, 24.

19. Prigogine and Stengers, *Order Out of Chaos*, 39.

20. Jacques Loeb, *The Mechanistic Conception of Life: Biological Essays* (Chicago: University of Chicago Press, 1912), 24.

21. Rupert Sheldrake, *A New Science of Life: The Hypothesis of Formative Causation* (Los Angeles: Tarcher, 1981).

22. See "A Book for Burning," *Nature* 293 (September 24, 1981), 245–246.

23. Rupert Sheldrake, *The Presence of the Past: Morphic Resonance and the Habits of Nature* (New York: Times Books, 1988), 99–102, 135, 175, 314.


## 7. PROUST'S BRAIN

1. Gore Vidal, "Calvino's Death," reprinted in *At Home: Essays 1982–1988* (New York: Random House, 1988), 220.

2. Sir James Frazer, *The Golden Bough*, abridged in one volume (New York: Macmillan, 1963), 43–52.

3. See Ovid's *Metamorphoses*, Book I.

4. Ernst Cassirer, *Language and Myth*, translated by Susanne K. Langer (New York: Dover, 1946), 3–5.

5. *The Upanishads*, translated by Swami Prabhavananda and Frederick Manchester (New York: Mentor), 29–33.

6. Karl Lashley, *Brain Mechanisms and the Intelligence* (Chicago: University of Chicago Pres, 1929).

7. Marcel Proust, *Remembrance of Things Past*, vol. 1, 51.

8. Wilder Penfield, *The Mystery of the Mind* (Princeton: Princeton University Press, 1975), 22–25.

9. Wilder Penfield and Herbert Jasper, cited in Richard M. Restak, *The Brain: The Last Frontier* (New York: Warner, 1979), 238.

10. Sir Charles Sherrington, *Man on His Nature* (New York: Doubleday, 1953), 184.

11. Proust, vol. 1, 50.

12. Proust, vol. 1, 845–860.

13. Proust, vol. 2, 783–790.

14. Roger Sperry, "Psychology's Mentalist Paradigm and the Re-

ligion/Science Tension," in *American Psychologist* (August 1988), 607, 609.

15. See *The Holographic Paradigm*, edited by Ken Wilber (Boston: New Science Library, 1982), 5–34; Karl H. Pribram, *Brain and Perception: Holonomy and Structure in Figural Processing* (Hillsdale, N.J.: Lawrence Erlbaum, 1991); and David Bohm, *Wholeness and the Implicate Order* (London: Arc, 1980), 1–26, 196–213.

16. Proust, vol. 3, 64.

## 8. THE SILENCE OF RIVERS

1. Novalis, "Aus den Fragmentensammlungen," *Gesammelte Werke* (Sigbert Mohn Verlag, 1967), 541.

2. Claude Lévi-Strauss, *The Savage Mind* (Chicago: University of Chicago Press, 1966), 16–22.

# Index


Abraham, Nicolas, 40
Agassiz, Louis, 78
Akhenaton, 2
Alexander the Great, 20, 40, 55–56, 58
Anthropic principle, 77
Archaeology, 5, 9–10, 13. *See also* Psychoanalysis
Aristotle, 7, 47, 55, 92
Arrian, 56
Astrology, 75–76
Asvaghosa, 54
Avery, Oswald, 100

Bachelard, Gaston, 85
Bacon, Sir Francis, 95
Bateson, Gregory, 91–92, 112
Bateson, William, 100
Baudelaire, Charles, 5, 9, 14, 18, 30, 94
Baudrillard, Jean, 105
Belousov-Zhabotinsky reaction, 89
Benjamin, Walter, 17–18
Bergson, Henri, 112
Bernstein, Jeremy, 55
Bertalannfy, Ludwig von, 112
*Bhagavad-Gita*, 46, 47–48, 51, 79
Boehme, Jacob, 99
Bohm, David, 128–129
Bohr, Niels, 50–51, 54–55, 95
Boileau, Nicolas, 81–82
Brain, human, 9, 84, 115–122, 124–125, 127–130
Breasted, J. H., 2–3
Brook, Peter, 48
Buddha, the, 16–17
Budge, Sir Wallis, E. A., 35–36
Butler, Samuel, 112, 114
Byron, Lord, 129

Cairns, John, 107

Calvino, Italo, 116–117
Camus, Albert, 103
Capra, Frank, 58
Capra, Fritjof, 55
Carnarvon, Earl of, 31
Carter, Howard, 23, 31
Cassirer, Ernst, 120
Cervantes (*Don Quixote*), 80–81, 83
Champollion, Jean-François, 25, 30
Chargaff, Erwin, 102, 108–109
Chopin, Frédéric, 115–116
Cicero, 60
Cinema, 32–34, 40, 58, 66. *See also* Hieroglyphics
Cities: unconscious, 8–9; unreal, 14–17
Clair, René, 32–33
Coleridge, Samuel Taylor, 43, 81
Crewe, F. A. E., 113
Crick, Francis, 100–103
Cuneiform, 25

Daniken, Erich von, 64–65
Dante, 15, 16
Darwin, Charles, 45, 90, 92, 100, 104
Dawkins, Richard, 96, 104, 105, 106, 108, 110
Democritus, 49
Derealization, 6–8, 10, 18–19, 20, 47, 52–53
Derrida, Jacques, 27, 34–36, 40–41
Descartes, René, 2, 50, 82–84, 95
DNA (Deoxyribonucleic acid), 95–97, 100–109, 110–114
Doolittle, Hilda (H. D.), 23–24
Dörpfeld, Wilhelm, 14
Dreams, 2, 12–13, 21, 29–31, 34, 80–84. *See also* Hieroglyphics

Einstein, Albert, 51, 68–69, 116, 130

Eisenstein, Sergei, 32–33
Egypt, ancient, 20–41, 56, 85, 133
Egyptology, 21, 23, 31–32, 38–39, 101
Ed Chatibi of the Harranites, 64
Eliot, T. S., 14–17
Eratosthenes, 38
Eternity, 13, 21–22, 32, 40, 45, 47, 63
Evans, Sir Arthur, 5
Evolution, 45, 84–86, 90, 92, 94
Existentialism, 3, 103–104

Fakhry, Ahmed, 38
Feagin, Jean, 107
Fibonacci progression, 87
Fliess, Wilhelm, 12, 13, 31
Forgetting, 2–3, 133. *See also* Oblivion
Frazer, Sir James, 116
Freemasonry, 56–58
Freud, 2, 6–10, 12–14, 15, 16, 17, 29–31,
    35, 39, 74–76, 125
Freund, Karl (*The Mummy*), 33–34
Frobenius, Leo, 19, 64

Galaxy, 60–64, 70–73, 76, 89, 125
Galla Placidia, 11–12, 64
Gaur, Albertine, 28–29
*Genesis*, 5, 24, 30–31, 45, 64–67, 96–98
Genetic engineering, 96
Gnosticism, 64–66, 76–77
Golding, William, 79, 92
Gould, Robert Freke, 57
Gribbin, John, 77
Grotefrend, Georg, 28–29

Hallucination, 11–12
Hannibal, 13
Hardenberg, Friedrich von (Novalis),
    132
Hawking, Stephen, 77
Hegel, G. W. F., 22, 26–28, 35–36, 37–
    38, 40, 46
Heidegger, Martin, 132
Heisenberg, Werner, 50–51
Heraclitus, 94, 96, 114
Herodotus, 20, 22, 24, 37, 40
Hieroglyphics, 9, 25–31, 32, 39–40. *See
    also* Writing
Hilton, James, 58
Hipparchus, 38
Holography, 66, 129

Homer, 5, 80, 91, 108

Imperialism, 20–21, 23, 33–34, 42–47,
    55–56
India, 14, 17, 21, 42–59
Individuality, 2, 52–53, 122–123
Irwin, John T., 22

Jaffe, Sam, 58
Jantsch, Erich, 93
Jasper, Herbert, 124–125
Jaynes, Julian, 40
Jesus Christ, 12, 22, 56, 115
Jonas, Hans, 64
Jones, Sir William, 42–45, 49
Joseph (Vizier of Egypt), 24, 30–31
Joyce, James: *Finnegans Wake*, 49–50;
    *Ulysses*, 61–63, 68
Julian the Apostate, 115
Jung, Carl, 2, 11–13, 15, 16, 17, 46, 64

Kant, Immanuel, 2, 70–76, 123
Karloff, Boris, 33
*Kena Upanishad*, 121, 122
Khufu, 20, 37–38
Kipling, Rudyard, 57–59
Kircher, Athanasius, 36
Koldewey, Robert, 5, 14
Kuhn, T. S., 106

Lashley, Karl, 121–122, 124
Le Corbusier, 87
Leibniz, Gottfried Wilhelm von, 26, 99
Leucippus, 49
Lévi-Strauss, Claude, 132
*Lingua adamica*, 99
Linnaeus, Carolus, 90
Loeb, Jacques, 109–110
Lovelock, James, 92
Lucretius, 49, 89, 90

McDougal, William, 113
*Mahabharata, The*, 48–49
Memory, 1–4, 11, 45, 52–53, 118, 121–
    130, 131–133. *See also* Myth
Miller, Stephan, 107
Milton, John, 80, 93
Modernity, 5, 16–19, 33, 43, 132
Monod, Jacques, 96, 103–104, 105, 108,
    110, 114

Mozart, 87
Myth, 6, 18, 19, 60–61, 89–92, 96, 120,
    126–127, 129, 132–133. *See also*
    Memory

Napoleon, 2, 20–21, 22, 37, 41, 55
Newton, Sir Isaac, 50, 98–99, 100
Nietzsche, Friedrich, 56

Oblivion, 131, 133
Oppenheimer, J. Robert, 2, 47–49, 51,
    53, 59
Overbaugh, Julie, 107
Ovid, 60, 90, 120, 126–127

Pascal, Blaise, 62
Paul, Jean, 13
Penfield, Wilder, 124–125
Plato, 7, 22, 56, 67–68, 77, 112, 117–118,
    132
Plutarch, 133
Pope, Alexander, 99
Pound, Ezra, 6, 8, 15, 16, 17, 19
Pribram, Karl, 128–129
Prigogine, Ilya, 89, 93, 109
Prophecy, 78–81
Proust, Marcel, 2, 123–130, 133
Psychoanalysis, 6–14, 18, 29–31, 40, 75–
    76
Pyramids at Giza, 20–21, 27–28, 36–41,
    65, 85, 87
Pythagoras, 38, 42, 56

Quantum physics, 50–55

Ramses II, 24
Rees, Martin, 77
Rilke, Rainer Maria, 60
Robinet, J. B., 85
Rutherford, Lord, 49

Sanskrit, 43–45
Santillana, Giorgio de, 68
Schlegel, Friedrich von, 36, 45
Schliemann, Heinrich, 5, 9, 10, 14
Schopenhauer, Arthur, 56
Schrödinger, Erwin, 2, 51–55
Seashells, 1, 78–93
Seeing, 119–120
Serres, Michel, 36–37, 89

Shakespeare, 63, 80
Shaw, Janet, 107
Sheldrake, Rupert, 3, 110–114
Shelley, Percy, 24–25
Sherrington, Sir Charles, 63, 125
Simpson, Larry, 107
Smyser, J. W., 82
Sperry, Roger, 128
Spinoza, Baruch, 56
*Sri Bhagavadam Purana*, 48–49
Stars, 1, 60–77
Steitz, Joan Artgetsinger, 106–107
Stengers, Isabelle, 109
Strachey, James, 75
Stuart, Kenneth, 107
Subiela, Eliseo, 66
Sublime, the, 2, 41, 72–74

Taoism, 54–55, 69
Thales, 36–37
Theatres, 32
Thom, René, 112
Thompson, D'Arcy Wentworth, 87–89
Thucydides, 22
Tintoretto, 61
Tompkins, Peter, 38–39
Torok, Maria, 40
Tutankhamen, 23, 31

Unconscious, the, 1–3, 6–10, 11–14, 18–
    19, 23, 33, 40
Underground, 5–6, 15–16, 17–18
*Upanishads, The*, 46, 51, 122

Valéry, Paul, 5, 14, 86–87
Virgil, 87, 108

Waddington, C. H., 112
Watson, James, 100–103, 105, 108
Weissman, August, 100, 111
Whitehead, Alfred North, 52, 112
Whitman, Walt, 115–116, 129
Whorf, Benjamin Lee, 53–54
Wilson, E. O., 105
Wincklemann, J. J., 13
Wordsworth, William, 2, 80–81, 83–84,
    88, 92–93
Writing, 28–29, 34, 117–119, 123, 132–133.
    *See also* Hieroglyphics

Yeats, 112, 114

Designer:    U.C. Press Staff
Compositor:  Impressions
Text:        10/12 Palatino
Display:     Palatino